PENGUIN BOOKS

DOCTOR IN THE NUDE

Richard Gordon was born in 1921. He has been an anaesthetist at a big London hospital, a ship's surgeon and an assistant editor of a medical journal. He left medical practice in 1952 and started writing his 'Doctor' series. He is a member of Surrey Cricket Club, and is married to a doctor. They have four children and live in a Victorian house in South London.

Richard Gordon's 'Doctor' books have been made into seven popular films and have more recently inspired a long-running television series which enjoys worldwide success. He has also published five novels on medical themes, the latest of which, *The Sleep of Life*, deals with the dramatic innovation of anaesthesia a century ago.

Doctor in the Nude

RICHARD GORDON

PENGUIN BOOKS

Penguin Books Ltd, Harmondsworth, Middlesex, England
Penguin Books Inc., 7110 Ambassador Road, Baltimore, Maryland 21207, U.S.A.
Penguin Books Australia Ltd, Ringwood, Victoria, Australia
Penguin Books Canada Ltd, 41 Steelcase Road West, Markham, Ontario, Canada
Penguin Books (N.Z.) Ltd, 182–190 Wairau Road, Auckland 10, New Zealand

—

First published by William Heinemann 1973
Published in Penguin Books 1976

—

—

Made and printed in Great Britain by
Hunt Barnard Printing Ltd, Aylesbury, Bucks
Set in Monotype Baskerville

I

'YOUR gracious Majesty – '

Sir Lionel Lychfield, FRCP, dean of St Swithin's Hospital, bowed solemnly and continued to an angle of some eighty degrees from the vertical. His expression – he had put much thought into his expression – was intended to convey at the same time loyalty untainted with flattery, a humility well short of cravenness, courtesy free from affectation and the self-assurance of a freeborn Englishman unmixed with impertinence. The dean felt he looked somewhat like Sir Walter Raleigh throwing his cloak across the puddle. But as he was a short, elfin-eared, quick-tempered man with a pointed bald head, he resembled a surly garden gnome hit in the back by the lawn mower.

'As dean of St Swithin's Medical School, Your Majesty, this afternoon it is my cherished honour, my most pleasurable duty, to present Your Majesty with this golden key, so that Your Majesty may most graciously declare this splendid new hospital building – this magnificent achievement of constructional science, consecrated to the highest ideals of humanity – well and truly open.'

The dean bowed a few degrees lower over his outstretched hands, appearing in danger of toppling on to the royal feet.

'We at St Swithin's, Your Majesty, take pride in our tradition of uninterrupted devotion to the sick, on this very site in north London, since the end of the sixteenth century. Our original Royal Charter – still to be seen in our Founders' Hall, which is said to be the work of Inigo Jones – was most graciously presented to the hospital by Your Majesty's forebear Queen Elizabeth the First. Much, Your Majesty, has been uttered by your loyal subjects in song, in story, in poesy, about our glorious heritage of tradition oh bugger it.'

The cause of the dean's annoyance was his wife's voice coming up the stairs. 'Yes, yes?' he shouted back. 'What is it?'

'You've a visitor, Lionel.'

'What, at this hour? It's barely seven o'clock and I'm still in the bathroom. Isn't even a man's morning toilet sacred?' He was standing, still bent at the middle, on his pair of clinical-looking scales, wearing only his gold-plated waterproof wristwatch and a large pair of round metal-framed glasses. 'What sort of visitor?'

'The hospital chaplain, dear.'

'Oh my God,' he muttered, inaccurately if flatteringly.

The dean straightened up. He was a consultant physician, his brain trained to illuminate instantly the most obscure diagnostic corners of the medical wards. He saw at once every possible reason for the call so early on a Thursday summer morning. Someone of national importance had died overnight in the private patients' floor. Or a patient in his pyjamas was on a twentieth-storey window-ledge and threatening to jump. Or the students had again put the reverend gentleman's motor-scooter on the chapel roof. Or there was another outburst of sectarian controversy with the reverend Roman Catholic father about the quality of the fish served for the patients' Friday dinners. Or the chaplain wanted him to read the lesson next Sunday in the hospital chapel. Or he was trying to raise money for a charity. All these conjectures the dean found equally repugnant.

'When I haven't even had a bite of breakfast,' he complained to himself, pulling on a yellow silk Paisley dressing-gown and sticking his feet into a pair of red and purple tartan slippers. 'If I hadn't responsibility enough looking after the patients' bodies. The bloody man might at least get on with his job of looking after the souls without calling in a second opinion.' He raised his voice. 'All right, all right, I'm coming.'

He hurried downstairs. He lived against the ancient walls of St Swithin's itself, in a tall pleasant house of vaguely Georgian style, the middle in a terrace of three. They had been recently built on the site of the hospital's old septic wards, mercifully made redundant with the discovery of antibiotics over the past forty years, and were let by the hospital to senior members of the consultant staff on the excuse that it would be handy to have them nearby for any unusually elaborate emergency. The dean being financially prudent – he was said by his students to make Scrooge look like a TV giveaway show – the modest rent appealed to him. But he recognized with irritation how the geographical position left him vulnerable to anyone from the hospital inclined to buttonhole him with a grievance.

The stairs led down to a narrow hallway, from which a door opened into the sitting-room, with its bow window, comfortably shabby furniture, shelves of books and the glass case of running cups which the dean had won as a student. The Reverend Osbert Nosworthy was inspecting myopically the dean's picture of eighteenth-century St Swithin's, said to be by Canaletto.

'Good morning, padre,' the dean began briskly. 'Splendid weather, is it not? So often July is disappointing. Nothing but rain and hail, ruining the crops and such things. You're looking very well. Extremely fit indeed. No medical complaints, I hope? And what can I do for you?'

He became aware of something strange about the chaplain, an elderly, paunchy, chinless man with untidy white wisps round the pink dome of his head. He customarily went about God's business at St Swithin's in a yellowish clerical collar, a black stock encrusted with the memorials of innumerable soups and a grey herringbone suit which the dean had often thought of incinerating as a sanitary hazard. But now he wore a check shirt, a scarlet and gold MCC tie, and an ancient green Donegal tweed jacket with grey flannels cut in the style of twenty years before, and carried a panama hat.

'Ah, Sir Lionel,' the chaplain greeted him jovially. 'I fear I have disturbed you at your morning ablutions. A thousand pardons.'

'Not at all. Though of course one is always extraordinarily rushed at this time of the day. I have alas hardly a minute.'

'I felt I just *had* to say goodbye to you.'

'How very kind.' The dean stuck out his hand. 'Well . . . goodbye.'

'I assure you that I have been trying to catch you at the hospital. For some weeks now. Perhaps months. I don't think I've even had the pleasure of congratulating you on your recent knighthood? But every time I call at your office, it would seem from your secretary that you are either out, or busy in committee or engaged in a consultation.'

'Really?' The dean tapped his finger-tips together impatiently. He was still at a loss why the chaplain should suddenly decide to haunt him. The Reverend

Nosworthy had been at St Swithin's since the dean was a medical student himself – looking the same age, and as far as the dean could remember wearing the same grey suit. But the dean could hardly recall exchanging a word with him apart from 'Merry Christmas'. He had no idea even what a hospital chaplain did. He believed the fellow spent his time cheering up the terminal cases and seeing all the books got back to the hospital library. 'It was kind of you to call.' The dean opened the sitting-room door.

But the Reverend Nosworthy seemed disinclined to move. 'I assure you I should have picked a more convenient hour, but my train is on the early side.'

The dean nodded towards the bow window, the cul-de-sac of Lazar Row outside already brilliant with morning sunlight. 'You've a nice day for it.'

The chaplain suddenly looked miserable. 'That makes my parting even less sweet sorrow.'

'Indeed? I should be delighted to be going on holiday myself. This year, I doubt if I shall do better than a snatched day or two in November. With my unending work on the new building. And of course the Queen.'

'I fear you misunderstand me. I am going for good. Retiring.'

'My dear padre – ' The dean shook him vigorously by the hand. He felt he could be limitlessly affable, now there was no possibility of ever having to speak to the man again. 'The hospital won't seem the same.'

'I have taken a room in a guest house on the outskirts of Whitstable. Where doubtless I shall spend my remaining days.'

'You out of one door, the Queen in at another, as it were.'

The chaplain shook his white hair. 'It's sad. I had

been rather hoping my appointment could have been extended a few weeks, so that I shouldn't miss so splendid an occasion. But my bishop was quite inflexible. Absolutely so. I even had the impression he thought I had been at St Swithin's far too long. The bishop is a very new broom, you know. And one accustomed to raising clouds of dust.'

'I'm sure you'll find Whitstable perfectly delightful, if a trifle chilly in winter.' The dean led his visitor firmly towards the front door. He was not anxious to become involved in the arcane complexities of Church politics. 'You must send me some oysters.' The chaplain looked blank. 'From Whitstable. There are oysters everywhere down there, surely? I am very fond of oysters in season, but of course they are too ridiculously expensive to eat in a London restaurant. I expect you can simply pick them up on the beach.' The dean shook hands again. 'Look after yourself. Make sure you register with a reliable local National Health doctor.'

The chaplain paused on the front step. 'I'm sorry that I couldn't introduce you to my successor. We somehow haven't overlapped. He's a much younger man than me – naturally so. A Mr Becket. Thomas Arnold Becket. The bishop certainly seems to think most highly of him.'

The dean made to shut the door. 'I'm sure the pair of us will get on splendidly.'

The chaplain put on his panama. 'Bless you, Sir Lionel.'

'And . . . er, the same to you. Good-bye.'

The chaplain lumbered down the flight of four stone steps to the pavement. He was shaking his head and mumbling about something. The dean fancied he caught the word 'Oysters'.

2

'OLD Nosworthy's apparently been put out to grass.'

The dean descended a few steps from the hallway to the large, bright kitchen at the rear of the house, on a level with a small garden lively with midsummer flowers. The well-shorn lawn ended at a high brick wall which had marked the limits of the hospital for centuries, but now there rose above it a brand new glass and concrete thirty-storey tower, which the dean's left-hand neighbour, Sir Lancelot Spratt, complained was ruining his roses.

'Though why the bloody man had to burst in here at day-break to tell me, I can't understand,' the dean added.

His wife Josephine, in a green housecoat, looked up from the electric stove. She was younger than him, pleasant, grey-eyed, soft-mouthed, ample-bosomed. 'But surely you knew, Lionel? Samantha and the rest of us at the League of Friends of St Swithin's got up a collection to buy him an inscribed silver salver. I gave five pounds from the house-keeping.'

'*Five pounds!*' The dean sat on a stool at the pink formica topped table, wrapping the dressing-gown round his skinny thighs. 'What's the League of Friends want to keep Nosworthy in silverware for, anyway? I thought you were mostly concerned with seeing the patients drew up their wills properly and got plenty of fresh fruit and that sort of thing.'

'Lionel, you do seem to grumble so much these

mornings. You should know by now that for years the League has taken responsibility for the hospital chapel. And since Samantha Dougal took over as our chairman, a very active responsibility, I might say.'

The dean said nothing. Josephine noticed he always fell silent and then changed the subject whenever she mentioned his sister-in-law. 'Well, I shan't be sorry to see the back of old Nosworthy. I can't imagine how many cases of cross-infection he caused in that suit. Though personally, I don't see why the hospital needs to spend money employing a chaplain at all. People should really understand by now that modern medicine is a strictly scientific activity. We have surely advanced somewhat since the days of the Black Death.'

'I'm sure it's a great inconvenience to you modern scientific doctors, Lionel, that your patients should persist in being the same old human beings.'

The dean grunted. 'Well it's my skill at scientific medicine rather than a soapy bedside manner which has won me . . . or which *will* win me this autumn, if all goes well . . . the job of . . . you know what.'

'Oh, Lionel!' Josephine suddenly looked at him admiringly, turning a switch under a boiling saucepan. 'How wonderful it will be – "Sir Lionel Lychfield, Physician to the Royal Household".'

'Of course, that's one down from your actual physician to the Queen,' the dean protested modestly. 'The doctor merely to the Royal Household doubtless has to enter Buckingham Palace by the back door. I assume one starts off by attending grooms and footmen and that sort of thing. But it's an enormous honour. Which like all honours in this country can of course lead somewhere.'

'To the *front* door?'

But the dean's mind had strayed. He had a vision of

himself at twelve-thirty on the following Thursday morning, in exactly a week's time. He was in exquisitely pressed morning clothes, gardenia in buttonhole, the cushion of purple velvet in his upturned hands bearing a golden key, all round him in the spacious marble-lined main hall of the new St Swithin's were assembled lords and ladies, medical mandarins from the Ministry of Health, grave-faced academics in gorgeous gowns, the most expensive doctors in the country and persons prominent in the local Rotary. His speech was still not *exactly* right, he had to confess. He had the words by heart weeks ago, but still needed perfection with the inflexions, the subtle pauses, the delicate emphases. . . .

'Your eggs, dear.'

'Thank you, Your gracious Majesty.'

'Lionel! I do wish you would try to live a little more in the same world as the rest of us.'

The dean opened the morning paper, looking flustered. 'Talking of Samantha, I see your brother's got a new novel out.'

Josephine sat on a stool opposite. 'Yes, he says these days the publishers' Christmas season starts during the summer heatwaves, like the football.'

The dean read aloud, ' "In *The Brothels of the Mind* Auberon Dougal scathingly indicts contemporary attitudes to sex and materialism. He calls messianically for man's rediscovery of innate human dignity, and a seeking of the salvation which lies in the self. The horizons of Mr Dougal's philosophy continue to expand, as may be readily perceived through its flatness".' The dean looked up. 'That was a nasty one, wasn't it?' He ended reading, ' "One can already see Mrs Samantha Dougal lending her dutiful if predictable support on television".'

'Auberon says the reviewers are all quite childishly jealous of him.'

'At least they seem to understand what his books are about. I can't.'

'Auberon's an intellectual, dear,' she told him gently.

'I'm not, I suppose? No one is, if they use their brains to do anything useful. Auberon always makes me feel like a plumber with bad breath and a smelly blowlamp.' He looked round as someone came into the room. 'Ah, Faith, my dear. Slept well? Missing the school bell and cold plunge, no doubt?'

'Good morning, father and mother. Yes, the first morning home from Horndean Hall is always delightful.'

The dean smiled tenderly, dipping a strip of brown bread and butter into the rich orange yolk of his egg. His seventeen-year-old youngest child was one of the few human beings unfailingly to stir feelings in a man so buttoned up emotionally as himself. His son George had amazed him by finding the wealthiest *au pair* girl in London and marrying her, turning himself into a jet-propelled executive – particuarly as the dean had in the boy's formative years written him off as half-witted. His elder daughter Muriel, now Professor Oliphant's house-surgeon at St Swithin's, had certainly inherited his brains, but his nose and ears as well. But with Faith – although her intelligence perhaps reflected too steeply the reversal to norm from his own brilliance – he felt that the genes of his wife and himself had been well shaken and thrown a double six.

Faith sat at the table. She was slim and fair, with large blue eyes, a small chin, a figure of geometrical neatness and a demure manner – which the dean, for one, found in a person of her age both unusual and heartening. 'I expect you're glad to see the last of Miss Clitworth's establishment?' he asked her heartily. 'Horndean Hall always struck me as a place where everything was regularly disinfected, including the girls' minds. Not that the fees weren't ruinous. Though I suppose if you can afford to send your children to snob schools,' he reflected, 'in this country it's the height of snobbery sending them to free ones.' He licked his eggy fingers. 'It's strange to think of you as no longer a schoolgirl.'

'She's been looking ridiculously mature in that horrible uniform for years,' Josephine told him.

'Mind, the way they let you carry on at Horndean Hall would have been thought quite scandalous in my own schooldays. Our only permissiveness was restricted to extra raspberry jam on Saturdays. But of course, then there were only girls and boys, who turned overnight into women and men, with none of this ridiculously self-conscious complication of teenagers – '

'*Please*, Lionel. Not your welcoming lecture to the new students again.'

'Nevertheless, Faith – ' The dean held a strip of dripping bread over his mouth like asparagus. 'You will have to turn your mind to your vocation in life.'

'I already have, daddy,' She had recently taken to addressing the world in a voice of husky solemnity, which lent dramatic quality even to the request for two lumps of sugar. The dean wondered if the girl had trouble with the larynx – a nodule, possibly, on the vocal cords. Perhaps she should be seen by one of his throat colleagues.

'Really? What?'

'I want to help people.'

The dean cracked his second egg with a decisive, wristy tap. 'Very praiseworthy. Though unfortunately the only examinations you have managed to pass are in needlework and cooking, and even the nurses at St Swithin's need A levels these days. Exactly why you want academic qualifications to put someone comfortably on a bedpan or serve a fruit jelly is beyond me. Heaven knows what Florence Nightingale would have thought. It's the fashion, I suppose. What was your favourite school subject?'

'Civic affairs. We learnt from Miss Clitworth all about the world.'

'H'm. Well, I'll arrange for you to make yourself useful in St Swithin's for a bit. To get the smell of the wards, as it were. You can start off by being the Queen.' Faith looked surprised. 'I'm holding a rehearsal of the opening ceremony at nine sharp tomorrow morning. You shall be Her Majesty's stand-in.' He gulped down his coffee and stood up. 'The work, the worry of it all! I seem to have hardly a moment for my proper function of treating the sick. I don't suppose you happened to hear any jokes in Horndean Hall, Faith? Perfectly respectable, but of course funny? No?'

'Surely there must be dozens of even respectable jokes going round St Swithin's,' suggested Josephine.

'Possibly. But I'm afraid that I am not the sort of man people tell jokes to,' the dean ended a little pathetically, going upstairs.

In his bedroom he donned bright purple briefs and a pair of green socks, wearing the Walter Raleigh expression supplemented with a smile which was respectfully restrained without being obsequious. 'But Your gracious Majesty is very kind.'

'Not at all, Sir Lionel. It was a most amusing little story.'

'I am deeply grateful for Your Majesty's approbation.'

'As you can imagine, over the years these opening

ceremonies tend to become just a teeny bit boring.'

'But I'm sure. I sympathize sincerely with Your Majesty.'

'And a little bit of fun helps everything along, don't you agree?'

'With all my heart, Your Majesty.'

'I really must tell it to the family when I get home.'

'That is extremely flattering oh bloody hell, what is it now?'

His wife was calling up the stairs again. 'You've another visitor, Lionel.'

'But it isn't eight o'clock yet! A man really can't concentrate on social niceties before he's digested his breakfast and opened his bowels. All right, all right, I'm coming.'

He pulled on his dressing-gown, replaced the tartan slippers and hurried downstairs. In the hallway, wearing his usual formal striped trousers and black jacket, was his neighbour Sir Lancelot Spratt.

'Morning dean,' the surgeon greeted him affably. 'Having a long lie in? Looks as though I shall have done a couple of gastrectomies before you're up and about.'

'What do you want at this hour?' the dean asked irritably.

'Just to remind you about the rugger club annual dinner at Luigo's Restaurant tonight.'

'I haven't forgotten. I'm picking up my houseman at St Swithin's about seven.'

'And also to remind you to take taxis. You've never been to one of these occasions, but they usually end up with the waiters having to barricade themselves in the kitchen. Never do to get breathalized in your nice new Rolls, eh?' Sir Lancelot jerked his head in the direction of the three garages opposite the houses across the road.

'I suppose soon you'll be having the Royal Arms and "By Appointment" on all the doors?'

The dean looked innocent. 'I don't understand.'

Sir Lancelot chuckled. 'Come off it, dean. Everyone knows you're in the running as quack to the Royal Household. I only hope you get it.'

The dean gave a modest smile. 'That's remarkably kind of you, Lancelot.'

'It'll be useful if I want some decent tickets for Ascot. By the way, I shan't be at St Swithin's for the skylarking next Thursday.'

'You won't?' The dean looked astounded. 'Why ever not? As senior surgeon, you're entitled to be right at the front.'

'Unfortunately, I shall be floating off the coast of Africa. I am going on a cruise. At six tomorrow morning I fly from Gatwick to pick up the ship at Tenerife. I could not of course ever miss the annual rugger dinner.'

'But you never told *me*!' The dean looked deeply affronted. 'Well, I hope you enjoy it. I myself certainly wouldn't risk a trip like that unless I was sure of someone reasonably sensible to talk to,' he added grudgingly.

Sir Lancelot stroked his beard, grinning. 'On the contrary, I am taking pains about not talking to anyone. I shall not let on that I am a medical man – the shipping line is certainly in complete ignorance of the fact. For once, I shall be able to relax and behave like a normal human being.'

'What a ridiculous idea.' The dean shook his head. 'You'll never be able to keep it up.'

'Why not? It's perfectly easy once I restrain our regrettable professional tendency to tell people continually that whatever they do in the line of eating, drinking or sex is probably bad for them.' Sir Lancelot opened the front door. 'By the way, it isn't penguins tonight. And I should put on your oldest suit. These affairs aren't half as rowdy as I remember them, when the evening wasn't thought complete without a raid on Bart's or Guy's. Now I suppose the students run amuck in the pursuit of high principles, rather than football trophies. But with the rugger club you never know.'

'Josephine!' called the dean urgently as the door shut. 'Sir Lancelot's slighting the Queen. He's off tonight on a world cruise.'

'How lucky.' She reappeared from the kitchen. 'I'm quite envious. Oh, I know we always have a lovely month every year at Swanage. But I've a mild suspicion there may be something interesting beyond.'

'But my dear! How can I possibly get time off for a world cruise?'

'Take a sabbatical year.'

'Let alone afford to pay for it?'

'Visit a few local hospitals and set it off against your income tax. Exactly as when you go fishing in Scotland. It's the same principle.'

The dean looked uncomfortable. 'Mind, if I'd paid for a world cruise and found myself in the same boat as Sir Lancelot Spratt, I'd either demand my money back or chuck myself into the sea, whichever afforded the quicker relief. I *must* get dressed. And if anyone else comes to the door, you can tell them that the levee is over.'

3

'WHAT was that quaint Scotch air the boys were singing, Lancelot?'

'*The Ball of Kirriemuir.*'

The dean's mouth had slipped from its normal line of petulant sanctity, and his customary air of ill-borne harassment by Man, Nature and the Fates replaced with a gaze through his large round glasses of Pickwickian benevolence. The rugger club dinner was traditionally held in a private room of a Soho restaurant, which the party had just noisily left for the street. 'Probably wise of you to break things up, Lancelot. After the extraordinary amount of draught ale the boys got through.'

'According to the author of *Jorrocks*, when men begin to sing it's a sign that they are either drunk or have had enough of each other's company. I didn't notice you stinting yourself particularly on the booze, either.'

'I happen to have a particularly hard head for alcohol,' said the dean with dignity. 'Always did.' He stopped short, pointing into a well-lit shop window. 'Those three girls on the cover of that magazine – what do you suppose they're trying to do?'

'I can't say exactly, but it's anatomically impossible.'

'Pornography, I suppose?' suggested the dean, still looking keenly.

'Pornography is an absurdly imprecise term, dean. It depends entirely on the personal standards of the individual. Like constipation.'

'That's odd – a strict German governess is advertising

for an interesting position. I imagined that sort of domestic job had quite disappeared from modern British society. What's this theatrical entertainment we're heading for?' he asked as Sir Lancelot tugged him away. 'Intimate revue, I take it?'

'Very intimate.'

'Do the boys know where it is?'

'Of that I have no doubt whatever.'

They strolled across the grid of garish Soho streets, in which the glow of artificial light always seems the more natural illumination than God's. 'Amazing area, this,' Sir Lancelot continued. 'A bit of everywhere else right in the middle of grey old po-faced London. Any atmosphere from Paris to Peking. Any appetite satisfied in a remarkable variety of ways. And at really quite moderate prices.'

'I know only the throat hospital in Golden Square.' the dean told him. He became aware of his new house-physician beside him, in his best suit. He was a pale, earnest-looking young man with a large head, and glasses which always seemed to be slightly askew on his face. 'Ah, Undercroft,' said the dean heartily. 'Do *you* happen to know a funny story?'

'Yes, sir.'

'Excellent. Tell me.'

'Well, there was this patient, sir, who had a glass eye.'

'Go on,' said the dean encouragingly, as they crossed Old Compton Street.

'And he swallowed it, sir. So he went to his doctor, who decided, because of the symptoms, he'd better perform a sigmoidoscopy.'

'I see. Yes?'

'And when the doctor had got the sigmoidoscope well and truly in, sir, the patient said, "Can you see anything?" And the doctor said, "No". And the patient said, "That's funny, because I can see you".'

The dean laughed loudly, then abruptly stopped. 'I'm afraid it would not do at all for the purpose I had in mind.' He looked round. 'What an awful lot of models seem to live about here. It must be the photographic centre of the country.'

The two consultants followed the dozen or so young men up a narrow brick-walled alley into a cul-de-sac, where street-cleaners were clearing the remains of the day's open air market. Crushing underfoot squashed tomatoes and decaying lettuce, the dean found himself hustled through a small lighted doorway. Unexpectedly, he was standing in the darkness of a hot, smoky, unusually small theatre, blinking towards a dimly-lit stage about the size of his own breakfast-table, on which a pretty, plumpish girl in an Edwardian gown with a bustle was twirling a parasol and singing *Daddy Wouldn't Buy Me A Bow-Wow*.

'Old time music hall,' smiled the dean to Sir Lancelot beside him. 'Quite delightful. Pretty voice she's got.' He frowned. 'She's not opening her mouth. Must be a ventriloquist, too. How clever.'

'The singing's all recorded on tape, you fool.'

'Really? How remarkably complicated.'

The rhythm changed to a calypso. The performer furled her parasol and started taking her clothes off.

The dean swallowed.

'Good God,' exploded Sir Lancelot.

'Yes, it is rather shocking – '

'Look at that appendicectomy scar. Someone's been at the poor girl with a bulldozer.'

'She *is* rather obese, don't you think,' observed the dean thoughtfully.

'In parts.'

'Do you often come here?'

'Don't be ridiculous. The boys seem to like it after the rugger dinner.'

'I'd imagine they'd see enough naked bodies at their work.'

'There are bodies and bodies.'

'Indeed.' The dean looked with interest as the girl removed her frilly long Edwardian drawers. 'It *is* a little reminiscent of gynaecological out-patients.'

'There's clinical nudity and erotic nudity.'

'You know, the difference has never occurred to me before. I say, she's got her wristwatch on. And a gold cross round her neck.'

'If *you* were stripping to the buff in a place like this, you wouldn't leave anything in your pockets.'

The girl was then wearing nothing but an artificial red rose, which with a pleasant smile she tossed into the audience. 'Lovely arse,' came an appreciative murmur in the dean's other ear. 'You could crack walnuts with it.'

As he turned, startled to find this emanated from his mild-looking house-physician, the lights went out. The audience rose as a man. The dean grabbed Sir Lancelot's arm. 'The police! I'm ruined.'

'Calm down, dean! It's everyone trying to grab the front seats, that's all. I should imagine the members of our scrum have done pretty well.'

The lights went up again. There were two girls on the stage, one giving the other a bath.

'Though I find the asymmetry of that young woman's patellae absolutely absorbing,' said Sir Lancelot, 'a little of this goes a long way. We'll leave the boys to it.'

'Oh, I don't know. I'm finding it – exactly, terribly boring,' agreed the dean quickly.

They pushed their way out. 'The pubs are still open,' observed Sir Lancelot. 'We might find an amusing one for a nightcap.'

But as they reached the entrance of the alleyway the dean found his shoe stuck in a rotting cauliflower. While he struggled to kick himself free, a woman's voice exclaimed, 'Lionel! What a delightful surprise.'

He looked up, into the large hazel eyes of his sister-in-law, Mrs Samantha Dougal. 'Oh! Hello.' He searched round wildly. For a man of his bulk, Sir Lancelot had melted amazingly away. 'I seem to have this cauliflower on my foot.'

'What an encouragement it is! That you too have become interested in this sort of thing.'

'Is it?' The dean tried desperately to reassemble his normal expression, but somehow his facial muscles refused to co-ordinate. 'What sort of thing? Oh, *that* sort of thing. Are *you* interested in it? How surprising.'

'But of course I am, Lionel. The appalling concentration of nudity and pornography in this tiny area . . . all unleashed in the name of liberalism, progress and liberty. Driving our Christian civilization remorselessly to servility and sterility . . . didn't you see my programme last week?'

Mrs Samantha Dougal looked at him with concern in the lamplight. The woman who preached so persuasively from the television screen, whose newspaper articles sharpened the bleakness of countless breakfast-tables, whose letters to *The Times* could make even clergymen feel ashamed of themselves, whose firm step heading a delegation to Downing Street was said to make the Prime Minister take refuge in the Treasury, resembled more nearly Miss World than Mrs Grundy. She had high cheekbones, a splendid skin, full lips, eyelashes like the teeth of a rake, and long bright auburn hair – so effective on colour sets – which she usually let tumble to her handsome shoulders but was now confined in a silk headscarf. 'Are you quite well, Lionel? You don't seem at all yourself.'

'Bit muzzy.'

'Muzzy?' She looked even more solicitous. 'Why should you be muzzy?'

'Slight temperature – doubtless summer flu.'

'Poor Lionel.' She patted his shoulder gently. The dean thought even more keenly than usual what a remarkably splendid woman his sister-in-law was. She patted him again. He made a note to feign minor illness every time he met her in future. 'You should be at home and in bed, Lionel. Not in the rank shadows of the new dark ages of depravity, into which two thousand years of civilization are collapsing. But I suppose you wanted to see for yourself?'

The dean nodded. 'Wanted to see for myself. And I saw.'

'*What* did you see?' she asked with professional interest.

He waved a hand vaguely. 'Oh, things. Girls smoking in the street. You know.'

She drew a printed sheet from a bundle under her arm, pressing it into the dean's hand. 'Take this. It's a transcript of my TV programme the Sunday before last. I'm sure you'll find it thought-provoking.'

'Thanks. Ever so.'

'Well, It's only a week now until our great day at St Swithin's.' The dean swallowed. Even the Queen was out of his mind. 'By the way, I do hope you can meet the chaplain tomorrow,' she added.

'Impossible. He's in Whitstable.'

'I mean the *new* chaplain. The bishop laid great weight on my advice when appointing him, you know. After all, I *am* the Chairman of the League of Friends. I'm sure you'll find the young man most stimulating. And now I must be about my work. I have all these papers to give away in drinking clubs and similar sad places before catching the last train back to Guildford. Give my love to Josephine.'

'Oh! Yes. By the bye . . . you needn't mention to Josephine we met.' Samantha's eyes grew larger. 'She wouldn't like to think of me in such dangerous haunts. I might get my throat cut any moment, surely! You know how she does rather mother me.'

'Of course, I won't say anything which might worry her, Lionel. Good night.'

The dean scuttled away. He screwed up Samantha's tract and threw it into a convenient dustbin. He was perhaps ridiculously touchy about such brief indignities as visiting strip shows, he thought. But Sir Lancelot would be out of the country by breakfast time. Nobody else was likely to split on him. There was no reason why his wife should ever know. And after all, he thought more cheerfully, she never got to know of the afternoon he spent with his staff nurse, locked by the students in a two-foot-square clothes cupboard.

4

AT nine o'clock promptly the next morning, despite a hangover, rubbing his hands in eager anticipation of his day's activities, the dean marched briskly with his daughter Faith towards the plain plate-glass doors of the new St Swithin's Hospital.

The doors slid aside at his approach – doubtless due to some mechanism concealed under the doormat, the dean supposed. He rather enjoyed the novel sensation. It was akin to being bowed in by flunkeys. This satisfaction had been hardly marred at all by the two or three occasions when the apparatus failed to work, and he had banged into the glass with his nose.

The dean was a more open-minded man than his students suspected. He could still alternate between the youthful view that all change is to the good, and the middle-aged one that all is too good to change. But he felt the new St Swithin's would take some getting used to. He was always a little surprised every morning to see it still there. But the old buildings had been quite dreadful – yellow-bricked, slate-roofed, narrow-windowed, massively-doored four-storey blocks, as forbidding as a jail, strung on an endless flagstoned corridor of dankness and gloom, as remembered for ever by those whose footsteps had ever rung in it. It had all been paid for by public subscription, and charity is notoriously hard-faced in bestowing its bounties.

The old forecourt was still there, separated from a shopping street as busy and as ugly as any other in outer

London by the same row of stout spiked railings, brightly repainted, to which the politically more active students attached their banners and sometimes themselves in support of each currently fashionable cause. The Inigo Jones Founders' Hall had been preserved, suggesting under grey London skies the canopied gondolas and gold-threaded brocades of seventeenth-century Venice. Also the hospital chapel, exuberant in red brick, stained glass and polished brass, erected by hard-headed Victorian merchants who saw no reason why the house of God should be less substantial than those they were building for themselves in the better residential suburbs. Here the voice of the Reverend Nosworthy had been raised against the forces of evil regularly at eleven o'clock every Sunday morning for forty years. The rest of the buildings had vanished, making way for another which, with the years – the dean thought in his more humble moments – would come to be equally scorned as ugly, inconvenient and inhuman.

As the dean entered the wide, low-ceilinged, rather too richly decorated main entrance hall, his enthusiasm for the new building took a sudden leap. It dropped again abruptly. The professor of surgery was waiting for him.

'Ah, dean – '

'Morning, Gerry. Well now, let's get on with the rehearsal. No time to waste. We've less than a week to get everything absolutely perfect.'

'Dean – ' persisted Professor Gerald Oliphant, wrapping his shining white coat round his spindly frame.

'By the way, Gerry, you never told me old Nosworthy was retiring.'

'I'm sure I did. Anyway, I put you down for ten

pounds for the silver fruit basket the hospital gave him. I'd appreciate your cheque some time. Now listen, dean – '

The dean suppressed a choking noise. 'Right, ladies and gentlemen. Overture and beginners, please, as I believe they say on the boards at this juncture.'

He was addressing a crowd of about thirty, mostly in white coats, all showing little enthusiasm. They were students and housemen who had responded to a notice from his office, inviting their impersonation of the bigwigs to be assembled on the hospital's great day. They had come partly through curiosity, and partly through the rumour that free drinks and an official lunch would be involved in it somewhere. They had been joined while waiting by a couple of hospital porters, half a dozen patients in dressing gowns on their way to X-ray, and two families passing the time until the wards opened for visiting.

'Dean! Will you please pay a little heed to what I'm trying to say?'

The dean turned resignedly. Professor Gerald Oliphant was a tall, lean, dark-eyed, hawk-nosed man with luxuriant moustache and sidewhiskers, and an expression as cold as a deep-frozen prawn. The professor was not at all sure that he liked the new building. And the dean was not at all sure that he liked the professor.

'I used to be dean of the medical school myself once, so I realize your difficulties. But you are also chairman of the building committee. And as such are perhaps aware that this place, although it might do very well as a luxury hotel, contains certain defects as a hospital. In the two brief months since it became fully operational – '

'I do wish you wouldn't go on about it,' the dean told

him impatiently. 'At this stage we can hardly put the old buildings back, however much you might want to.'

'You misunderstand me. Admittedly, the former wards were built in the year which saw the Charge of the Light Brigade. Admittedly they survived attack by Zeppelins, the Luftwaffe and George Bernard Shaw. Admittedly our masters in the Ministry of Health, though landlords of several acres of clinical slum, were seen to wince noticeably over their teacups when anyone mentioned St Swithin's – '

'Can't we have all this later?' The dean tapped his foot impatiently. 'Now, ladies and gentlemen. My daughter Faith will play the Queen. The Duke. . . .' He searched for a fittingly commanding face. 'It will have to be you, Undercroft,' he directed his house-physician, that morning looking paler than ever. 'Go outside with my daughter.'

'Yes, sir. What do I have to do, sir?'

'Come in again.'

'Yes, sir.'

'When I give the signal, naturally. Off you go.'

'Dean,' Professor Oliphant interrupted perseveringly. 'I am also aware that the old hospital was replaced with one twice the size, that the cheapest route for expansion is into thin air and that your committee commissioned an architect of enormous fame and ingenuity, who has designed the most expensive places to be sick in from Seattle to Sydney – '

'*Please*, Gerry. Now I want a purple velvet cushion. Has anyone got one? I mean got any sort of cushion. Very well, we shall have to make do with this instead, I suppose,' he conceded as somebody handed him a steel kidney-dish.

'Nor am I insensitive, dean, to all we have endured for

the erection of this clinical gin palace.' Professor Oliphant seemed oblivious of anything in the hall except his own voice. 'As half the district would have been dead if they'd waited for those fancy new doors to open, we have witnessed the most interesting competition between clinicians and constructors. I'm not complaining that brick dust got anywhere from my theatres to the patients' dinners. That we had record wound infections and prescriptions soared for tranquillizers. That the labourers stole from the doctors' bedrooms by day as persistently as they peeped into the nurses' by night – '

The short fuse of the dean's temper was sizzling. '*Must* you waffle about all this now?'

'Waffle?' The Professor's voice took a metallic tone. 'We looked on this building with the vision of a better life hereafter, like the medieval poor with their new cathedrals. And doubtless we shall find ourselves equally disappointed. This surly, unsociable, uncooperative building does nothing but play malicious tricks on us. It *hates* us. The air-conditioning either blows a hurricane or attempts mass asphyxiation. The vast new car parks have followed an inflexible rule, and already become inadequate – '

'Now, the golden key. What can we use for the golden key? I suppose that's roughly the same size,' he agreed grudgingly as the gynaecology house-surgeon handed a gleaming speculum from the pocket of his white coat. The dean placed the instrument in the kidney dish, and with a respectful look balanced it across his upturned palms.

'Furthermore, dean – ' The Professor towered over him, eyes gleaming. 'I have been stuck in the passenger lift so often, I refuse to use it in future unless equipped with crampons and ropes.'

'It's no good complaining to me. Complain to the architect.'

'The architect's in bloody Peking. Building exactly the same hospital out there, God help the suffering Chinese.'

'Why *must* you always be so sarcastic?'

'Me?' Professor Oliphant looked more amazed than affronted. 'I've never used a sarcastic word in my life. Have I?' he appealed to the crowd, who had been enjoying the argument as an unexpected diversion from dull duty. Getting no reply, the professor wound his white coat round him again. 'I'll leave you in your self-appointed role of Cecil B. De Mille – '

'It's lucky that at least one of us on the staff can see his duty of providing Her Majesty with a fitting reception.'

'Duty? Amateur theatricals! When you were a student, we had to give you the tenor lead in the Gilbert and Sullivan every Christmas, or you'd sulk till Easter. *I* at least have some work to do. Good morning.'

The professor strode off. The dean stood glaring after him, muttering. Looking down and seeing the kidney-dish and speculum still in his hands he was brought back to business. 'All housemen to the right of the main entrance,' he commanded. 'All students to the left. When at the end I invite three cheers for Our Queer Dean – ' Everyone laughed. 'You know perfectly well what I mean,' he told them crossly. 'Where's my daughter got to?'

The dean stepped through the glass doors. He shouted. No reply. He dispatched the gynaecological house-surgeon, who finally produced them from among the parked cars in the forecourt. The dean waved his handkerchief. The automatic glass doors slid open. Faith and Dr Undercroft entered slowly, looking grave and holding hands. 'Good God,' cried the dean. 'You've arrived to open a hospital, not to get bloody married in Westminster Abbey.'

Faith looked at him reproachfully. 'Clem thought we'd look more stately like this.'

'Clem? Which Clem? What's Clem got to do with it?' Faith inclined her head towards the houseman, who now had the uneasy look of a small boy egged on to fight the school bully. 'Your name's *Clem*? Good gracious. How extraordinary. Well, I don't want any overacting.' The dean continued his stage directions, 'You will walk in quite naturally, Undercroft, a pace behind Faith. Then you will pause with an interested expression as I present her with this.' Clem stared at the instrument in the kidney-dish. 'This is merely a prop,' the dean said impatiently. 'On the night I shall have a golden key. Out you go again.' He turned to the rest of his cast. 'Everybody in their places? Right. Curtain up.'

Faith and Clem Undercroft again approached the automatic glass doors, but this time they refused to open. The dean tugged at them, breaking his nails. He sent someone to telephone the hospital engineer, but he was somewhere in the middle of the shaft trying to get Professor Oliphant out of the lift again. Then one of the visiting children was sick on the terrazzo floor, the cleaners were found to be on strike, and the dean decided to abandon the rehearsal for the morning.

5

'WELL, my dear Sultan, and how are we today?' It was ten minutes later, with the dean – as so often – masking bad temper under his feverish bedside manner. 'Undercroft, the notes.' The dean stood scratching his chin. '*Undercroft!* Notes.'

'Oh! Yes. Certainly, sir.' The house-physician had been staring with his mouth open through the window. They were on the twenty-eighth floor, two from the top. This layer of the new hospital was allotted to the rooms of paying patients. They had prudently taken one of the service lifts.

The dean flicked through the clipboard of different coloured papers. 'Quite comfortable, I hope, Sultan?'

'Delightfully. I had no idea your hospitals were so luxurious. Like your hotels, but the service is so much better and the young ladies much prettier. I shall recommend all my friends to stay in London hospitals rather than in London hotels. Money is, of course, no object with them.' The Sultan brushed his thick black moustache. 'I gather your Queen is calling next Thursday morning? I wonder if I might enjoy a few words with her? After all, she and I are in the same line of business, are we not?'

'I expect Her Majesty will be somewhat occupied.' The dean scribbled a note. 'We'd better have another blood urea done, Undercroft. *Undercroft!* What *is* the matter with you this morning? You seem half stunned.'

Undercroft shut his mouth. 'Oh. Yes. Sorry, sir.'

'A glass of champagne, Sir Lionel?'

'Very kind, but somewhat early after breakfast.'

'My religion of course precludes alcohol. But fortunately I enjoy among my powers that of making dispensations. Those grocers Fortnum and Mason are really excellent. Their caviar is so much better than what the Russians send me.'

'Anything else you require, Sultan, just ask this young man here. Undercroft!' The houseman jumped. 'Have you fallen into a catatonic trance, or something? I must now get upstairs to my office. We'll soon have you up and about again, Sultan, never to worry.'

'Don't forget about the Queen. I am not entirely uncertain that we are not related.'

Abandoning his oddly-behaving houseman, the dean took a couple of flights of the stone stairs that ran beside the passenger lift shaft, to the thirtieth floor above. There was a swing door at the top with a pane of glass set in it, marked EMERGENCY EXIT. The stairs opened on to a broad corridor, at either end of which picture windows gave startling views over the gloriously eccentric London skyline. As the dean pushed the door open, immediately to his left were the sliding doors of the lift on which Professor Oliphant seemed to have such an unsettling effect. Further to his left down the corridor were the professor's suite of offices. The dean's were at the other extremity on the right. In between, opposite the lift, was the psychiatric clinic. Professor Oliphant suggested it found itself in such a remote spot because the famous architect had completely forgotten about it, and had to stick it in somewhere before he put the roof on.

The dean opened the door of the outer office, where his pretty blonde secretary was typing. 'Good morning, Miss Duffin.'

'Good morning, Sir Lionel. Another enormous folder of letters and reports for you this morning, I'm afraid.'

The dean took the file from her with a sigh. 'Committees, committees . . . these days I seem to see more angendas than anginas.'

She smiled. 'Rather good, Sir Lionel.'

He smiled back. 'Thank you. I can't understand why the students say I have no sense of humour.'

He entered his own airy office, shutting the door. He sat at his stylish teak desk. For a moment he stared at the pile of papers. Then he felt in the bottom drawer, producing from a hiding place under reprints from medical journals a small green-covered book, on its cover a gold serpent twined round a winged staff, the doctor's international trademark.

The dean stood up. He held the book stiffly in front of him. He cleared his throat. '*Ouvrez la bouche. Vous avez de mauvaises dents.* Open your mouth. You have bad teeth. *Comment fonctionne l'intestin? Depuis combien de jours n'êtes-vous pas allé à la selle?* How many *days* haven't you?' he muttered. 'A constipated lot, those Frogs. Wouldn't have thought so, with all that garlic.'

The dean had like all British doctors an intense suspicion of medicine as practised beyond the Channel. It was obviously over-influenced there by the kitchen and the Church, and anyway conducted in an atmosphere of great excitability. But he recognized grudgingly that St Swithin's like the rest of the country was now in the European Community, and having dutifully invited several new-found colleagues from Europe to the Queen's opening he felt he should equip himself with a little clinical patter.

'*Prononcez "Ah"*. Say "Ah". That's easy enough, anyway. *Le crachoir*, the spittoon. Ugh. *Avez-vous eu*

la syphilis? Combien de fois? What an extraordina depraved crowd those French patients must be. *de la blessure*, where were you wounded, yes Miss Du what is it?'

'There's someone to see you. A Mr Becket.'

'Becket? I don't know any Becket. Is he one of t new students?'

'He could be. He says he's anxious to get straig down to work.'

'Well, I'm certainly always glad to encourag keenness. Show him in.' The dean dropped the phras book and stood with outstretched hand. '*Bonjour.* Gooc morning, that is.'

The visitor was a skinny young man about his own size, athletic-looking though pale, with dark brown hair down to his shoulders, prominent greenish eyes and a thick pointed beard. He wore frayed jeans and sandals, a white singlet and a green anorak. The dean was not particularly startled. In a world where most of the younger inhabitants appeared to be on their way to a fancy-dress ball, he realized sadly the day had passed when a student appearing in a tweed jacket could be asked cuttingly where he had left his golf clubs. 'Take a pew,' the dean invited.

'Thanks.'

The dean sat behind the desk, finger-tips together. As the visitor said nothing, he observed as amiably as he was capable, 'This clement weather doubtless suggests casual wear. But I hope you will adopt a little more conventional attire before appearing in the wards.'

' "What went ye out for to see?" ' The voice was pleasant, with a Cockney tang. ' "A man clothed in soft raiment?" '

'I beg your pardon?'

'Matthew eleven, verse eight.'

The dean shifted uneasily in his new padded leather chair. This was clearly the pious sort of student, who needed watching. He had noticed a regrettable tendency for preoccupation with spiritual matters to be one of the earlier manifestations of mental instability. 'I see you are somewhat religious.'

'And you are perfectly right. Are you?'

'Of course.' The dean looked offended. 'I invariably read one of the seven lessons at the hospital carol service each Christmas.'

'And that discharges your debt to God for the year?'

'Well, I've had no complaints,' the dean told him stiffly.

'I'll certainly offer the annual chance to clear your conscience against next Christmas.'

The dean sat up with a start. 'Becket! Of course. Why, Mrs Samantha Dougal was talking about you only last night, when I ran into her outside that strip – outside that poodle-stripping parlour. But I must say, I hardly expected a clergyman of the Church of England to walk into my office in his undervest.'

The Reverend Becket was not put out. 'The disciples never decked themselves in new clothing.'

'Possibly. But the disciples hadn't the advantage of Marks and Spencers round the corner.' The dean sat fiddling with his papers, uncertain what to do. He didn't want to interfere with the hospital chaplain. Indeed, he hoped completely to avoid contact with him, from one Christmas carol service to the next. But he could hardly condone any hospital functionary whatever strolling through the brand-new wards in trousers which seemed to have paid too many visits to the launderette. 'If you are a little short of ready cash – doubtless

you give lavish alms to the poor and such people – the hospital social workers,' he suggested, 'keep a small wardrobe of clothes left by patients who have died. You will find the garments in good repair and thoroughly fumigated.'

'Well, it's the living who need charity more than the dead, I suppose?'

The dean caught the chaplain's eye. It made him feel uncomfortable, as though he were steadily breaking his way through the Ten Commandments. 'I take it you have some idea of your duties, Mr Becket? I certainly haven't. Though I expect some official circular has been issued by the Ministry of Health on the subject of hospital chaplains. They have issued a vast number on absolutely everything else.'

The Reverend Becket smiled. 'You don't think I should be guided by the word of God?'

'As far as the Ministry are concerned, the two are synonymous,' the dean told him crisply. He straightened his papers. 'But whatever your duties happen to be, I am sure they are pressing. So I shan't detain you any longer. Please don't hold hymn-singing sessions in the wards. It always seems to upset the sisters. Good morning.'

When his secretary returned from showing Mr Becket out, the dean explained quiveringly, '*That* if you please was old Nosworthy's successor.'

She gasped. 'But he looks as though he slept in the park.'

'Oh, he probably did. It's quite distressing how these long-haired layabouts infiltrate everywhere these days, even the Church. I may be old fashioned, but I was brought up expecting the parson to wear a dog collar, have short back and sides, be good at cricket and mention God only on Sundays. Please understand, Miss Duffin, that Heavenly hippie is not to be allowed in my sight again. Not in any circumstances. Is that clear?'

'*Quite* clear, Sir Lionel.'

'And should I unfortunately succumb in the hospital at some future date, Mr Nosworthy is to be called back specially from Whitstable to bury me.'

6

SHORTLY after six-thirty that evening, the dean hurried into his house in Lazar Row, dropped his briefcase and black homburg in the hallway, strode purposefully into the sitting-room and with a key from his pocket opened a small triangular cupboard in the corner. He drew out a decanter of sherry and two glasses. Suddenly, he paused. Sweat broke out on the nape of his neck. Supposing the automatic glass doors failed to open in response to the royal progress? Supposing the rest of them were inside the building – all the notables, himself pathetically holding out the golden key on a cushion at the front – with Her Majesty making frantic signals to be admitted? He must order the hospital engineer to lock them open for the ceremony, he decided. There was doubtless some mechanism for this. But supposing the building with its customary malevolence, he continued to imagine with horror, managed to shut them with a snap just as Her Majesty was passing through, threatening to divide her longitudinally into two Majesties? 'Cor,' he said.

'Lionel! What's happened?'

He looked up to see Josephine inspecting him with alarm from the doorway. 'Nothing, nothing. I've had a worrying day, that's all.'

'Me too. I spent a perfectly torturing afternoon with the League of Friends of St Swithin's. I think this evening I need a whisky.'

'Whisky? *Est-ce que vous croyez que je suis construit d'argent?*' His wife looked blank. 'French,' he explained.

'I'm trying to improve my vocabulary for these Frogs, Krauts, Wops and our similar brothers from Europe.' With another key he opened his wooden microscope case on the bookshelf, and extracted a bottle of scotch with a syphon.

'Samantha would have come round, but she's gone home to Guildford,' Josephine apologized, taking her glass. 'She said she's sorry not to see you, as you haven't met for simply ages.'

'But what rubbish. I met Samantha only last – last February, how time does fly.' The dean sipped his sherry. 'Samantha's new hospital chaplain blew into my office today. He looked in urgent need of a square meal, a barber and an ecclesiastical tailor.'

'You've met him!' Josephine's face lit up. 'Isn't he sensational?'

The dean glared. 'What have *you* been hobnobbing with him for?'

'He addressed the League of Friends this afternoon. We found him tremendously sincere and absolutely captivating.'

'But he walks about in his underclothes.'

'You're simply prejudiced. You should admire the Church for keeping up with modern society. The medical profession doesn't even try.'

The dean wagged a finger. 'I take the greatest exception to that remark, my dear. It is surely an undeniable fact that no-one has a deeper understanding of human beings than their doctors.'

'Only when they're ill, Lionel,' she corrected him gently. 'Which you tend to forget is not the normal condition in which everybody cares to spend their lifetime. I have anyway invited Mr Becket to lunch on Sunday.' The dean scratched his right ear with his left hand across the top of his bald head, his habit in moments of extreme vexation. 'And you are not to give him the Beaujolais you won in the students' raffle, but the claret you got from that gouty bookmaker.'

'Why should I fill my house with freaks and weirdies, ordained or not? Just when we've got rid of that perverted psychiatrist Bonaccord from the house next door, too.' The dean jerked a disdainful thumb in the direction opposite to Sir Lancelot's. 'I reckon Bonaccord was so kinky you could have catheterized him with a corkscrew. Ah, good evening, my dear.' He was aware that his daughter Faith had entered the room, as usual as unobtrusively as a winter shadow.

'Good evening, daddy. Good evening, mummy.'

'Now that you have been freed permanently from the genius tutelary of a ladies' seminary. . . .' The dean hummed a few bars of *The Mikado*. 'I think you are entitled to a glass of sherry in the evening.'

'I should *love* one, daddy.' Faith's voice had the thrilling, dramatic quality of Cleopatra soliloquizing to her asp.

He poured a small glassful. 'Cheer ho, my dear. Or chin chin, as we used to say when I was your age. Not of course that I was allowed to drink a glass of sherry at your age, any more than I was allowed to visit low theatrical performances with naked women.'

'What an extraordinary choice,' said Josephine.

'But times are changing violently. I suppose today, with three children, your mother and I can be accused of biological pollution.'

His wife drained her whisky. 'Perhaps it was a good thing I lost the baby we were going to have last autumn. When Sir Lancelot was having all that fuss with Dr Bonaccord. We should have been rather elderly new parents, shouldn't we? We're better off waiting for our three to pollute the world further with grandchildren.'

'Possibly, possibly . . . I suppose you haven't remembered a funny story yet, Faith?'

The dean poured himself a second glass of sherry, not keen to reminisce over a painful incident. Sir Lancelot had three funny stories, of course, which he insisted on telling at every hospital dinner and which the dean long ago knew by heart, but they were far too outrageously anatomical. Everyone else he had asked in the hospital seemed only to know the one about the sigmoidoscope and the glass eye. He might even approach Professor Oliphant . . . the dean recalled he hadn't seen the professor all day, and wondered idly if he were out of the lift yet. He remembered the Reverend Nosworthy had a funny story about St Peter and the pearly gates to cheer up patients on their death beds, but that seemed rather specialized. Perhaps the new chaplain could provide one? the dean wondered. But no. He didn't seem the jokey type.

'I don't think Miss Clitworth had a great sense of humour, daddy.'

'That was the precise impression I – ' The doorbell rang violently. 'Good heavens. It can't be Sir Lancelot back already? See who it is, Faith.'

They heard the front door burst open. There was a gasp. A groan. An anguished cry of, 'For God's sake! Help me!' An instant later there staggered into the room a tall, craggy, fashionably dressed, youngish looking man with carefully arranged copper coloured hair, his right hand carrying a large briefcase and his left clutching his chest. 'I'm dying.'

'Auberon!' Josephine jumped to her feet. 'But what happened?'

'I'm dying. Dying! Where can I sit down?'

Josephine laid her brother gently on the sofa, loosening his green velvet bow tie and the collar of his coffee-coloured frilled shirt. 'Faith, fetch your father's emergency bag from his study. Auberon, you poor boy ... are you in pain?'

'Pain? Bloody agony.'

'Where?'

'All over. I feel terrible. God! To be struck down, just like this! Someone telephone my agent. I've got to appoint my literary executor.'

'We must reach Samantha in Guildford – '

'No, no! Don't distress my poor wife. Besides, I shall probably be dead before she can get here. The trains are terrible this time of the evening.'

'Lionel!' Josephine looked up, on her knees beside the moribund author of *The Brothels of the Mind*. 'How can you just stand there, with that awful smirk on your face? Won't you do *something* to save your brother-in-law?'

'No.'

'How can you be so heartless?'

'Because I can diagnose without bothering to put down my sherry that nothing in the slightest is wrong with him.'

Auberon jerked up his head. 'Then what's this awful pain round my heart?'

'Wind. It was on the last half dozen occasions you were dying. Dissolution seems to be a chronic complaint with you.'

'This time I may really be *in extremis*,' the author complained hotly. 'That'll make you look silly.'

'Of course, if you're not satisfied with my opinion, I can have you admitted to the wards of St Swithin's in the care of the Professor of Surgery.'

'Ugh! No.' Auberon Dougal looked alarmed. 'You

know how hospitals give me the creeps. Just lying there on your back, waiting for people to come and do nasty things to you. Horrible.' He propped himself on an elbow. 'Perhaps I'm not so bad as all that.'

Faith reappeared from the dean's first-floor study with the black leather case in which he kept phials of emergency drugs and syringes. The dean continued to sip his sherry. Auberon was a younger man than himself, of course, he reflected. One must make allowances. But he didn't like him. The dean didn't know precisely why. It may have sprung from the ingrained opinion of all Englishmen that authors are as a class incorrigible if enviable idlers.

'We must put you to bed,' said Josephine tenderly. 'I'm sure I've remembered enough of my training at St Swithin's to nurse you properly.'

'Which bed?' demanded the dean. 'Or do you intend your brother to ruin our own night, by performing his death rattle lying between the pair of us?'

'We've still the little room at the back, Lionel. The divan's small, but perfectly comfortable.'

'I'm far too ill to take much notice of my surroundings,' Auberon told her.

'*Mon dieu,*' muttered the dean. '*Parbleu.*'

Auberon noticed the whisky bottle. 'I think a drink would do me better than anything.'

'Faith, pour some of your father's whisky into that medicine glass in his bag.'

Auberon suddenly became aware of his niece. 'It can't be? Not little Faith? You *have* developed, haven't you?'

'I was doing a lot of gym at school, uncle.'

'Then Lionel can drive his new Rolls to Guildford and bring Samantha back.'

'Not much point, really.' Lying on the sofa, Auberon gulped down a medicine glass full of whisky and stretched out his arm for more. 'I've left her.'

The dean began to look interested.

'But you and Samantha seemed such a particularly well-matched couple,' exclaimed Josephine.

'Oh, it doesn't take a great effort to avoid throwing things at one another in public.' Auberon drained a second glass and passed it to Faith for a refill. 'Then this morning she accused me of writing potboilers. Potboilers! *The Brothels of the Mind* a potboiler! You might as well say *Lady Chatterley* was a handbook for gamekeepers. Oh, I admit freely the days are gone when authors were actually recognized in the street. When they had dishes named after them in fashionable restaurants. Like haddock Arnold Bennett – haddock and pimentos, quite disgusting.' He swallowed another glass of whisky. 'It's depressing, but writing novels today is only the last of the cottage industries.'

'But Auberon, your books appeal only to the most discerning of readers,' Josephine consoled him.

'Oh, yes. They could hold a seminar on my work, the lot of them, in any reasonably sized saloon bar. *And* the bastards get them all out of the library, anyway. Can't blame them, I suppose,' he continued with sudden sad resignation. 'Who'd fork out the price of a couple of bottles of gin for a hardback book? When they can wait six months for the paperback, at the price of a pint of beer? I think my pain's coming back again.'

'Faith, give your uncle another drink.'

'But Samantha, now! She's got it made,' Auberon continued. 'Since she's been on the telly, Guildford has been all over her. No one takes a damn notice of me. I'm just her husband. Mr Samantha Dougal. As a lot of people have discovered in this country from John Wesley to J. Arthur Rank, public morality can be a good business. Besides, she's always going on about the sanctity of marriage. I'm fed up with the bloody sanctity of marriage. With Samantha, I keep wondering whether I'm going to bed or going to church. And now she's taken to compost-grown stone-ground bread, rose hip jam and biological mince.' He gave a loud burp. 'That's much more comfortable. Can I have another whisky?'

'You have behaved quite despicably to poor Samantha,' said the dean suddenly. Everyone looked at him. 'I mean, nothing is more mysterious than the marital upsets of other people,' he added vaguely.

'Do you feel strong enough to get down a little food, Auberon?' asked Josephine, smoothing the lapels of his plum-coloured jacket. 'You must keep your strength up, whatever the crisis in Guildford.'

The author looked more cheerful. 'Perhaps I could manage a little dinner. Nothing too heavy. I had an extraordinarily good lunch with my publisher at the Ritz Hotel.'

'*The Ritz Hotel*,' muttered the dean. 'What extravagance!'

'All London publishers lunch at the Ritz Hotel,' Auberon told him. 'It's a tribal instinct.'

'It will be nice to enjoy a little intellectual conversation for a change.' Josephine rose from beside the sofa. 'The League of Friends of St Swithin's will be terribly thrilled to hear you're staying with us. Many of them are quite literary, you know, and go regularly to the Foyle's lunches at the Dorchester Hotel. They say they always feel so secure at meeting only the most respectable type of author there. Lionel, you can ring Samantha and put the situation to her.'

The dean jumped. 'Me? Why?'

'You're always saying that half the art of medicine is sorting out the relationships of other people. Obviously, poor Auberon can't. He's emotionally exhausted.'

'Exactly,' Auberon agreed. 'And I'd quite forgotten – I left a cab outside. Can someone pay it off? I'm sure it would be dangerous for me to move.'

'Of course, Auberon. Faith, get some money from my handbag.'

The dean looked heavenwards. 'Everyone has gone absolutely *fou*.'

He felt confused, irritated and isolated. How do you telephone a lady you admire and respect to say that her worm of a husband has crawled from under the marital stone? How do you get rid of the husband, anyway? How do you prevent his ruining you by drinking crates of your whisky? How do you tell your wife forcefully that you haven't forgotten how her young brother Auberon set fire to your trousers while you were making a speech at your wedding? And furthermore that his books are a load of pretentious old codswallop? If only he had a friend – some sound, sensible friend – he could turn to for advice. . . . The dean swallowed. He never in his life imagined that he would miss Sir Lancelot.

Some three hours later, Sir Lancelot Spratt in his white dinner-jacket was leaning on the rail of the boat-deck, gazing over the moon-dappled water, listening from below to the soft eternal swish of the ship's progress and from behind to the faint strains of an old-fashioned waltz, holding in his left hand a balloon-glass of liqueur brandy and in his right that of a large-bosomed well-coiffeured lady whose diamonds twinkled attractively in the ship's fairy lights.

'But Sir Lancelot, what do you *do*?' He felt her curiosity had a flattering tinge of excitement. 'You were quite the mystery man, coming aboard at Tenerife this morning.'

'I am a farmer, Mrs Yarborough.'

'Do call me Dulcie. One of the charming things about shipboard life is everyone becoming so friendly and so equal, don't you think? And anyway, I shan't be Mrs Yarborough much longer.'

'Oh?'

'No, my divorce becomes absolute the day we cross the Equator. Isn't that a coincidence? So you're a farmer. I might have guessed. I can just imagine you, striding out with the dawn across your rolling acres of wheat and barley.'

'I happen to be a pig farmer.'

This silenced her for some moments. 'It must be very interesting.'

Sir Lancelot raised the brandy to his lips with a hand which had explored twenty thousand abdomens. 'Did you know the remarkable number of diseases to which pigs are liable, Dulcie? Quite apart from swine fever, they are subject to infestation with three entirely separate species of worm.'

'I'm afraid that I haven't had very much to do with diseased pigs,' she said dully.

'There is the large round worm – *ascaris lumbricoides*. Then there is the lung worm. And the red stomach worm, which though small is always found in profuse numbers. Would you like me to describe the symptoms?'

'No, I . . . I expect you're on this cruise for a complete change.'

'How right you are,' he agreed heartily. 'As a matter of fact my pigman suffered from depression all week and alcoholism on Saturdays, until last weekend when they coincided and he hanged himself in the sties. So I sold the pigs for sausages and came away.'

'But how terrible,' Dulcie Yarborough frowned. 'You know, I've been wondering who you reminded me of. An old vet who was used by my first husband.'

'I assure you, Dulcie, that I should faint at the very sight of blood.

Her other hand fell casually on Sir Lancelot's arm. 'You are a widower, I believe?'

He raised his eyebrows. 'How did you guess?'

'Oh, I happened to find myself in the purser's office this morning, and I suppose I must have casually glanced at one of the official ship's papers. Yes, steward?' she added with annoyance.

A man in a white jacket with a small silver tray stood beside them. 'Cable for you, sir.'

Drawing half-moon glasses from his top pocket, Sir Lancelot read the message. He tore it up and scattered the pieces on to the sea. 'No reply.'

'Something about your pigs?' asked Dulcie.

'No. From an old friend of mine. Alas, he was always a man of unstable temperament. Now he would appear to be off his head.' Sir Lancelot stroked his beard. 'Would you care to dance, Dulcie? I believe a Strauss waltz is still within my capabilities.'

7

THE dean woke.

'Oh! Your Majesty. I really am most terribly sorry.'

'Lionel, I have been sharing the same bed with you now for twenty-odd years. I am perfectly used to you kicking me when you are waking up. You seem quite unable to regain consciousness without some sort of convulsion. But there is no need to apologize so profusely.'

The dean blinked. He stared with relief at Josephine on the familiar pillow beside him. 'It was horrible. Terrible. My dream. So vivid. We were all waiting in St Swithin's for the Queen . . . Professor Oliphant, the Minister of Health, you, me, everyone – '

'But you *always* seem to be having that dream nowadays.'

'I know. But this time it was different. None of us had any clothes on.'

'Oh, those sort of dreams are far too common to relate.' Josephine found her husband's mental maraudings at night remarkably boring.

'Very strange, the psychology of dreams,' the dean mused. 'I might pop next door and ask Dr Bonaccord's successor about it. Not that I would ever have mentioned my dreams to Bonaccord himself – he was as nutty as a squirrel's nest, even for a psychiatrist.' The dean sat up, as the incoming tide of memory swept over the sand castles of the night. 'Oh, my God. We've got your brother Auberon staying with us. You really must get rid of the fellow today.'

Josephine looked at him coldly. 'Where to?'

'Back to Samantha, of course. After what she said to me on the phone last night. That he leaves her regularly, every six months.'

'Auberon's a sick man.'

'My arse. He's as fit as Cassius Clay in his prime.'

'Lionel dear, you *are* becoming vulgar. I don't know what your students think. Anyway, he wants to borrow your typewriter and have somewhere quiet to work. He always does three hours regularly before lunch. He says it's the only way. Self-discipline is the key to literary success – apparently Tolstoy, Flaubert and all those people had a great deal of it. Though at the moment Auberon is suffering from blockage.'

'I recommend liquid paraffin and phenolphthalein.'

'*Mental* blockage. It makes him feel quite suicidal.'

'I can't understand why you fuss over him. His is an entirely trivial occupation compared with mine. Anyway, I'm sure I could write any number of novels myself, if only I had the time.' The bedside telephone rang. 'Yes? Sir Lionel Lychfield here.'

'This is Gerry Oliphant.'

The dean winced. The voice always put him in mind of an old gate swinging in a windy night. 'I'm in the middle of my morning exercises.'

'And I am just in the middle of my breakfast. Dean – do you speak German?'

'No, I haven't got as far as the German yet. I'm finishing off French this week.'

'French is unfortunately no use with Herr Professor Doktor Stuttsenburg, because I've tried. It evokes only a clicking of the heels. Like a machine gun. It's getting on my nerves.'

'But these bloody foreigners – I mean our distinguished confrères from Europe – shouldn't be arriving to stay in your house till next week.'

'Exactly. In your preoccupation with playing Buttons in the royal pantomime, you would seem to have boobed.'

'The secretarial arrangements have gone haywire since we moved into the new building,' muttered the dean.

'Indeed. And while on the subject, my personal shower in the operating suite, though equipped with an ingenious series of lockers, has some unfortunate misconnection of the plumbing. It attempts every time I use it to remove my entire dermis with scalding water.'

'I'll look into it.' The dean tried to put down the telephone.

'The laundry chute from my theatres is excellent, but why does it always have to return only nurses' aprons? And why is the coffee in the staff dining room invariably boiling, and that in the students' cafeteria invariably stone cold? While the exact opposite holds for the soup?'

'I'll see what I can do.'

'Though you may be consoled to know that the meat loaf in both establishments retains exactly the same nastiness which I can remember as a student. The Herr Professor Doktor is clicking his heels again. I'd better go.'

The dean dropped back the telephone. 'I think, my dear, I shall have my boiled eggs in bed this morning. I really don't feel strong enough to face Auberon.'

An hour later, the dean crept downstairs silently. As he seized his black homburg and slipped out of the house, he could already hear the desultory tap of a typewriter from his own study. Auberon Dougal sat in one of the dean's week-end sweaters slowly composing.

Page I

THE TRUTH ABOUT ROSALIND

Chapter One

Waking that morning in late September, the freshness reminded me that men can tire even of summer, yet beguiled how near approached the narrow days of winter. The sun was a copper dish in a gauzy sky, while in the vallies brides' veils of mist twined suspended and motionless.

He stopped. So far so good. He sat scratching his ear, gazing through the window at the sunlit back garden, joyful with colour. He shook his head slowly. It was the twenty-eighth time he had written that paragraph. He'd counted every one. Sometimes the mist was in wraiths, sometimes the sun was a burnished medallion, sometimes it was October, and sometimes it was nightfall in the tropics. The paragraph was all right, as far as it went. The trouble was, he didn't know what to put next.

Auberon's eyes strayed down to the dean's black leather emergency bag. How nice to follow some secure, lucrative, creatively undemanding occupation like medicine! he thought. His well-exercised writer's imagination instantly saw himself in glistening white operating gear, busy on the white-draped body, his foot-long scalpel flashing in the powerful lights, his admiring audience a packed house of delightful nurses. *Forceps . . . swab . . . scalpel . . . now for the transplant . . . easy nurse . . . don't lose your nerve . . . there, fits like a glove . . . and the donor was my own son. . . .*

The lights changed. A television studio. Charming yet authoritative, he gave the lovely girl interviewer his views on transplants, surgery, sex, absolutely everything. The fee was going to be enormous. *That was all most interesting, Professor. Would you possibly have time to continue the discussion over dinner . . . ? But of course . . . Would my flat suit you? So much quieter. . . .*

Auberon sighed. Such a pity that the smell of disinfectant made him sick.

He was suddenly aware of not being alone in the small room.

He turned in his chair. The door was ajar. An eye regarded him solemnly through the crack. 'Faith? Do you want anything?'

'I'm sorry, Uncle Auberon. But I've never seen a real author at work before.'

He smiled indulgently, just like the transplant professor to his interviewer. 'Come and take a closer look, if you wish.'

Faith came in, shutting the door behind her. 'It must be wonderful being a novelist, and affording so much pleasure to millions,' she said breathlessly.

'It isn't. It's exactly as Oscar Wilde described landowning. It gives one position and prevents one from keeping it up.'

She looked puzzled. 'But Daddy always says you're loaded.'

'Oh, I *live* in style, admittedly. To quote Somerset Maugham, it's unnatural for an artist to live in a semi-detached villa and eat cottage pie cooked by a maid of all work. Samantha's the one who's well breeched. I'm skint. Do you know, even the people who write fan letters take my books free from a library? Which is like praising the head waiter for the food and service and departing without leaving a tip,' he ended sourly.

'Poor Uncle Auberon.' Faith looked meltingly sympathetic.

She *has* grown a big girl, he reflected. Someone

seemed to have attached a nozzle somewhere and inflated her. 'Last time I saw you, Faith, you were wearing a straw hat and a pillowcase made of gingham, and looked as sexless as a lamp-post.'

'Miss Clitworth at Horndean Hall has been giving us very thorough deportment lessons, uncle. When I started with the library trolley, going round the wards yesterday morning, the very first patient borrowed your book *The Electric Nasturtium.*'

'Excellent taste.' Auberon cheered up instantly.

'But he died during the afternoon.'

'What a pity. The best part of that novel is the ending.'

'I've got all your novels in my room, with the Bible and the Guinness Book of Records.'

'All my life's work.' He decided to paddle again in the black pool of his misery. 'I have said everything I can to the world. Perhaps the world hasn't listened particularly sympathetically. It may, when all that is left to hear are echoes.' He made a mental note to include that in his next book. A professional writer, like a professional chef, can afford to waste nothing.

'But Uncle Auberon, you've *years* to live yet. You're not as old as *that*.'

'Who knows?' Another vision came to him, lying like the seventeen-year-old poet Thomas Chatterton in the Tate Gallery, pale and twice as handsome in self-inflicted death. *That* would teach Samantha a lesson. His toe indicated the dean's emergency bag. 'This house must be stuffed with the most remarkably dangerous drugs.'

She breathed the words. '*You wouldn't?*'

He saw two tears run down Faith's peachlike cheeks. 'No man can be deprived of the last of human rights – the right to kill himself.' Auberon added, with great relish.

Faith unexpectedly leant forward and kissed him tenderly on the lips.

She drew back. She gasped. 'Did you mind, Uncle?'

There was another pause. 'Er . . . no, of course not,' he said, startled.

'It was the only way I could express my sympathy to the full.'

'Well, it's a. . . .' Auberon was still taken aback. 'A very nice way.'

'Shall I do it again?'

'If you like.'

It was going to be wonderful. He saw it already . . . the neglected, misunderstood, mentally suffering artist, revived by the pure love of a sweet young girl. A mixture of *Old Curiosity Shop* and *Lolita*. Of course, she was his own niece. It was a little irregular. But he seemed to remember some other well known public figure had enjoyed quite an affair with his pretty young niece. Who was it, now? Ah, yes. Adolf Hitler. 'H'm,' said Auberon. 'Perhaps you'd better leave me to get on with some work.'

She was looking over his shoulder. 'That's very, very beautiful, what you have written.'

'You think so?' He brightened again.

'But you've spelt valleys wrong, and the first sentence starts with a hanging participle. Goodbye, Uncle Auberon. Tonight I shall pray for you.'

He was alone. He ripped the sheet from the typewriter and crumpled it into the dean's wicker wastepaper basket. He tapped again.

Page I

THE TRUTH ABOUT MIRANDA

Chapter One

Waking on a morning in early April, the young girl sensed a freshness which beguiled how near had passed the narrow days of winter, yet proclaimed how close approached the summer from which men never tire. The sun was a yellow balloon in a cotton-wool sky, while in the valleys misty, muslin-like veils hung motionless. . . .

8

AT that moment one of Auberon's novels – *The Rubber Woman* – lay in the palm of Sir Lancelot Spratt. In orange T-shirt, knee-length khaki shorts and long white socks, he had strayed after breakfast into the ship's library. This was a nook off the promenade deck, in which he had already earmarked the deep leather chairs and well-supplied writing desks less for the pursuit of culture than as refuge from talkative fellow-passengers. He had drawn Auberon's book from the shelf on no more literary stimulation than having met the author a couple of times with the dean, and wondering if he would strike him as quite so inane in print.

'Can I help you, sir?' asked the library steward, in the hushed tones considered appropriate by the public in the presence of large numbers of books or a dead body.

'Have you anything on pigs?'

'Pigs, sir?' The steward looked worried. 'I can't say there's much of a call on board for books about pigs.' He thought a moment. 'But I've something on *guinea-pigs*.'

'That will probably do equally well. It is simply a matter of scale.'

The steward searched his shelves. 'The last ship's doctor presented it to the library, sir. He used to keep guinea-pigs in his surgery down below.'

'I am delighted that he had an experimental turn of mind.'

'Oh, he didn't *experiment* on the poor little things,

sir. He'd never have harmed a hair of their hides, if that's the expression. He said they were his only friends on board, sir. He used to talk to them quite a lot. Then one voyage he said they'd grown the size of elephants and were chasing him up and down the ship's alleyways. Dear me! What a to-do *that* was. We had to put him ashore into an institution in Peru. He's still there, for all I know. Though I don't suppose he'll be very comfortable, from the look of it. It's very strange, sir, the effect the sea has on medical gentlemen.'

'Very.'

The library door opened. 'Lancelot – there you are. I've been searching for you on deck. I never thought you were a bookworm.'

'There is nothing more restful after a heavy day on a pig farm than curling up with a good book, I assure you, Dulcie. Send that particular volume down to my cabin, steward,' he ordered. 'And now, Dulcie, perhaps you would join me in a drink? I should imagine the sun is over the yardarm. From the bar hours, the yardarm on this ship seems highly adjustable.'

As they strolled the few yards to the ship's smoking room she said, 'Lancelot, may I ask you something really outrageously personal? How did you achieve your knighthood?'

'I bought it.'

'Bought it!' She looked aghast.

'It's perfectly simple, if you know the right people. And knighthoods are remarkably reasonable. Compared with a life peerage, which I thought rather too pricy. I think you'd find that any titled persons you happen to know got theirs for nothing more than hard cash.'

'No!'

'Indeed. Naturally, I can't breathe any names, but obviously many of our public figures with titles could never with any stretch of imagination have got them on their own unaided abilities.'

'Now you mention it, that strikes me quite forcibly.' She paused while they sat at a table in the smoking room. Sir Lancelot ordered from an attentive steward a gin and tonic for her, with a Highland malt for himself. 'Whereabouts do you live in England, Lancelot?'

'North London,' he said absently.

'That's a very unusual place to have a pig farm, isn't it?'

'It's a battery pig farm,' he explained quickly. 'In an old warehouse. Most interesting. Pig farmers come from all over the world to see it.'

'But don't the people living all round object to the smell?'

'I have perfected the odourless pig. Perhaps you read about it in the *Pig Gazette?*'

'You *do* seem a most remarkable man.'

Before he could respond gracefully, a constrained voice over his shoulder announced, 'Sir Lancelot Spratt, isn't it? The charming Mrs Yarborough I already know, all the way from Southampton. May I introduce myself? I am Dr Ivo Runchleigh, the ship's medical officer.'

Leaning over him, fingers at cap-peak in smart maritime salute, in glistening white uniform with gold braid and scarlet stripes on his epaulettes, was a tall, thin, sun-tanned man who instantly reminded Sir Lancelot of the St Swithin's matron's parrot. He licked his lips. 'I am a pig farmer.'

'A most interesting vocation, I'm sure.'

'I know nothing whatever about medicine and surgery and all those sort of things.'

'And a very good idea, too.' The ship's doctor gave a superior smile. 'All that is very much better left to we doctors. Nothing is more disastrous than a meddling patient. As Jonathan Swift said, a little knowledge is a dangerous thing.'

'He didn't. He said a little learning was. And it was Alexander Pope.'

Dr Runchleigh looked for a brief moment disconcerted. Then he swept off his cap, to reveal a silvery well-groomed head. 'I'm sure you don't mind if I join you?'

'What's your poison?' asked Sir Lancelot uninvitingly.

'Of course, we medical men are obliged to keep a clear head at all times. It would never do to be under the influence. Eh, Mrs Yarborough? One never knows when one might be called on some errand of mercy.'

'Are you quite comfortable, Lancelot? You're wriggling about in your chair.'

'It's just an itch on the sacrum – on the bum.'

'But I see the steward has brought my usual, anyway,' explained the ship's doctor, as half a tumbler of brandy was set before him.

'Dr Runchleigh is really quite wonderful,' continued Dulcie admiringly. 'He treated me our first night out of Southampton for insomnia, and I've slept like a log since.'

'Oh? What did he give you?'

'Laudanum,' interrupted the doctor.

Sir Lancelot spluttered. 'You don't use bloody leeches still as well, I suppose? I mean,' he added hastily, 'do you medical people still use leeches for drawing blood?'

The ship's doctor laughed. 'Dear me, no. You *do*

have an old-fashioned view of our modern miracles.'

Sir Lancelot wondered why Dr Runchleigh's way of speaking gave him the impression of having a mouthful of red hot aniseed balls. 'Where did you qualify, doctor?' he asked.

'At High Cross Hospital in London.'

'High Cross!' Sir Lancelot guffawed. 'They turn out a right batch of prick-farriers – I mean,' he broke off, as Dulcie laughed. 'We in pigs tend to call doctors that. It's a term of affection.'

'I have never come across it,' said Dr Runchleigh, a little coolly. 'Are you enjoying good health abroad, Sir Lancelot?'

'Never fitter. Though I fancy I might have some slight salmonella infection – gut rot, that is – which might be expected in any closed community.'

The ship's doctor darted out his fingers to pull down Sir Lancelot's lower eyelid. 'H'm. Dear me.' He looked solemn. 'I'm afraid that we have a tendency to anaemia.'

'Balls. I mean, indeed?'

Dr Runchleigh nodded. 'Anaemia.' He looked even graver. 'Pernicious. Though fortunately we doctors can effect a cure. It is performed with liver. I would advise you to eat plenty of the grilled liver at lunch.'

'*Grilled* liver by mouth!'

'Lancelot! Are you all right?'

'Just . . . just a little fit of the shakes. I thought the liver had to be given by injection – I've several anaemic aunties – but doubtless I'm wrong. Sorry I spilt my drink over you, Dulcie. Steward! Swab. I mean, mop.'

Dr Runchleigh leaned towards Sir Lancelot confidentially. 'So you suffer from fits?'

'I am a martyr to them.'

'I think it would be most advisable for you to consult

me. Come to the ship's hospital at five this evening. I'm afraid there will be – and I think I had better make this clear, to avoid any unpleasant misunderstanding later – a fee. The National Health Service stops at the gangway. But we shall be in good hands. We shall examine ourselves thoroughly, and we shall soon be much better.'

'It is really amazingly kind of you, doctor,' Sir Lancelot told him flatly, 'to go out of your way and warn me that I am suffering from anaemia – a disease which might well be fatal.'

'Fatal? Anaemia? Oh, dear me, no. But we shall have to look after ourselves during the voyage.'

'And also to suggest I make use of your services about my fits. I should like to offer in return a cut-price side of bacon, but unfortunately touting for custom is strictly forbidden by the Pig Marketing Board. Now if you will both excuse me, I shall walk round the deck to stimulate the ticker by filling the old bellows with ozone.'

9

'Bonsoir!'

AT six-thirty that evening the dean came as usual promptly into his sitting-room, rubbing his hands. It was a Saturday, but he had spent the whole afternoon in St Swithin's, continuing his organization of the coming visit. Now he had the pleasant anticipation of his glass of sherry, his dinner and an evening spent splashing red ink over his students' examination papers.

He paused, hands together. Faith was in a small chair, fingers demurely clasped on her lap. Josephine sat very upright on the sofa. From the expression on their faces they were waiting for the undertakers to bring the coffin down. 'What's going on?' he asked with a puzzled frown. '*Qu'est-ce que c'est's* up?'

'Auberon,' said Josephine. 'He's in a state.'

'Another critic called him the Savonarola of the suburbs, I suppose?' said the dean testily.

'He's threatening suicide.'

'What, because he's left Samantha? How ridiculous. If I'd escaped from my own marriage bed, I should be far more concerned slipping into another one than into my grave.'

'Lionel!'

'A purely theoretical illustration,' he added quickly. 'What's Auberon been saying, anyway?'

'He was asking Faith today where you kept the dangerous drugs.'

'But he *mustn't* commit suicide.' The dean looked

angry. 'Not here, anyway. Not with the Queen coming. It would look terrible. I'm sure they'd never make you doctor to the Royal Household if you have suicides on your own hearthrug. It could arouse considerable lack of confidence.'

'Faith said he was dreadfully serious about it. And I'm sure a man like Auberon would never distress an innocent young schoolgirl with such talk, if he weren't utterly earnest and desperate.'

The dean frowned again. 'Well, what can we do about it? I used to send anyone threatening suicide at St Swithin's to the Reverend Nosworthy. Though he used to talk to them about Heaven in such glowing terms, it only acted like the brochure of some package tour. As for this new fellow Becket, he'd probably drive them to murder as well. I suppose I'd better have a word with him, treat him as a clinical case.'

'By the way, Lionel,' Josephine remembered suddenly. 'You're coming to St Swithin's chapel tomorrow.'

'I bloody am not.'

'Yes you are. It would be highly discourteous, the dean of the medical school not attending the new chaplain's first service.'

'I go to chapel every Christmas, and it seems to maintain me on a highly moral plane for the rest of the year. I see no reason to overdo matters.'

'Mr Becket has reserved a pew.' The dean scratched his right ear with his left hand across the top of his head. 'And you are to wear one of your best consulting suits, not that awful ginger tweed thing you sport on Sundays, which I remember you wore on our honeymoon.'

'Uncle kissed me this morning,' said Faith quietly.

Her parents broke off the argument and stared at her.

'*Auberon* did, darling?' asked her mother, looking puzzled.

'Twice. Full on the lips. I was too frightened to resist him.'

'But surely in a purely avuncular way?' suggested the dean.

'No, daddy. He was looking very sexy. He was making noises like our dog when it smells the postman.'

'Good God,' exclaimed the dean. 'That brother of yours, Josephine – he's as perverted as Christmas pudding on a picnic.'

His wife sat looking deeply concerned. 'He's quite obviously mentally deranged, poor dear boy. Temporarily, of course. That must be why he left Samantha in the first place. These brilliant artists, we must remember, Lionel, haven't the flat, dull stability of people like you and me.'

'He must see a psychiatrist,' the dean declared firmly. 'That's it. It'll settle his hash in one go about suicide and sexual assaults on schoolchildren.' Like all the physicians at St Swithin's, the dean found the psychiatry department a useful ragbag, into which he could stuff headfirst any persons whose behaviour disturbed in any way the orderly running of the establishment or himself. 'Yes, definitely. We must treat him as an emergency. I'll arrange it this very night.'

'Hello, there!' Auberon burst cheerfully into the room.

'Faith dear,' said Josephine quickly. 'Come and sit on the sofa beside me.'

Auberon stood in the doorway, staring. 'Well! You are looking glum, the lot of you. On a Saturday night, too. The telly gone wrong, or something?'

Josephine instantly flashed a smile. 'Not at all,

Auberon. We were just saying how wonderful it was simply to be alive.'

'I want a word with you – ' began the dean firmly. Then he noticed Faith with a finger to her lips. Her imploring look told him to spare her already traumatized feelings by keeping silence over her uncle's sexual assault.

'Yes?' asked Auberon expectantly, throwing himself into Faith's vacated chair.

'Er – have a whisky.'

'That's very kind.'

The dean crossed to his microscope case, taking the key from his pocket. Auberon certainly struck him as one of the most cheerful intending suicides he had come across. A veneer, doubtless. With these creative people you could never tell their real feelings. Perhaps they didn't have any. They kept painting the emotions of fictitious people, he supposed, but the canvas below was a blank. 'We were just discussing how lucky we were, having a distinguished literary gentleman like yourself staying with us.'

Auberon looked startled.

'I hope that you will continue to delight your public for many years to come. Though not, of course, continuing to give us the pleasure of your company here.' The dean poured him a large drink. 'You have a lot to live for. Did you know, by the way, that most suicides occur in early spring? It has all been worked out most carefully from the Registrar General's annual statistics. Summer, where we are now, is the most unfashionable season to kill yourself. Interesting.'

'If grisly.' Auberon took his glass.

'Very few gardeners or civil servants commit suicide. And hardly any clergymen at all. Odd. You'd imagine that clergymen would have a much better idea than anyone else of exactly what they were letting themselves in for. Perhaps that's why. I've no idea what the rate is for authors.' The dean paused. He felt he was not doing very well. 'I think you should consult a psychiatrist.'

Auberon looked amazed. 'Me? But whatever for?'

'Because . . . oh, it does everyone a lot of good to consult a psychiatrist from time to time.'

'No thank *you*,' said Auberon firmly.

'It would really be remarkably convenient,' said the dean encouragingly. 'A St Swithin's psychiatrist is living right next door. Dr M'Turk.'

'What a Kiplingesque name!' Auberon grinned. 'You can hear the very wail of the bagpipes in it.' His imagination saw Dr M'Turk, all flaming red beard and violent tartan, smelling of whisky with hands like hams, a volume of Freud in his sporran, ready with Presbyterian scorn for his own miserable little psychological peccadilloes. 'No,' said Auberon.

The dean stamped his foot. 'You must.'

'But I don't want to consult a psychiatrist. I don't *need* to consult a psychiatrist. In fact, Lionel, I deeply resent your suggestion that I *have* to consult a psychiatrist. I may admittedly have married myself to Samantha, but I am not a madman.'

'Daddy meant to get material for a book, Uncle Auberon,' said Faith quietly.

'Ah!' He snapped his fingers. 'Now you're talking. Of course! I've never done anything like that. *The Ego and I*, that might not be a bad title . . . or *As You Like Id* . . . yes, that's a splendid idea. It could be good for a quite substantial advance from my publishers . . . '

His eyes took on a distant look, his author's imagination racing away. He saw the hardcover edition, the paperback rights, the rather more lavish American version littering the coffee tables of the Middle West, the American paperback deal, the film of the book, the dramatic version (repertory and amateur rights), the musical version of the play of the film of the book, the television series (with repeats at reduced royalty), the anthology rights, the serial in Australia, the foreign translation rights including both Serbo and Croat versions for Yugoslavia. . . . 'It's a *terrific* idea! How soon can I see this Scots brain basher?'

'I'll telephone right this moment,' the dean told him.

He reappeared to say that Dr M'Turk next door was free, and could spare Auberon half an hour before dinner. Two minutes later, the author was ringing the bell of the house immediately on their right in Lazar Row. The door was opened instantly by a tall, slim, oval-faced, wide-eyed female in a long purple caftan, gilt sandals, and a string of nut-sized wooden beads looped round her waist. Her pale blonde hair hung well over her shoulders, cut square in a fringe just above her eyebrows, and kept in place with a band round her forehead of greenish snake. She had a pale, smooth skin, and could have been any age from eighteen to thirty-eight.

'Dr M'Turk, please,' said Auberon, now feeling some trepidation.

'Yes.'

'I've an appointment to see Dr M'Turk.'

She opened the door widely. '*Do* come in,' she murmured.

Auberon's eyebrows shot up. 'You mean, *you* – ?' He stepped briskly inside.

She took his hand. 'This way,' she commanded.

They entered the sitting-room. It was exactly the

same shape as the dean's, but so filled with exuberant house plants it gave Auberon the feeling of macheting his way through a jungle. There was an uncomfortable looking wickerwork sofa, on which Dr M'Turk sat. She indicated the cushion beside her. Auberon obeyed, brushing aside trailing strands of Climbing Fig. Still not speaking, Dr M'Turk turned and held her face close to his.

The silence continued. Auberon gave a nervous laugh. He asked, 'Should I say, "Don't be a Freud, I'm only a Jung man?" '

She remained expressionless, holding him steady in her pale blue eyes. 'This is quite wonderful.'

He looked surprised. 'Oh, really?'

'When I glanced through the window this morning, and saw you coming out of that stupid little man's house next door – and he *is* a horribly stupid little man, particularly about this royal visit, which I, of course being an anarchist, shall boycott – I said to myself, "It can't be". But it was.'

'This morning when I was slipping out to have lunch with my agent at the Savoy Grill? I'm sorry, I never noticed.'

'For years I've been absolutely *burning* to meet you. Quite on fire. Since I read your first book – '

'*Bed and Butter*.'

'I felt from the very first page, *here* was a writer who did something to me. A tremendous thrill went through my *entire* body. It was quite physical. Absolutely orgasmic.' She put back her head and gasped.

'So glad you liked it,' murmured Auberon, starting to relax against the hard wickerwork.

'I read it under the beclothes with a torch at school.'

'Oh! Of course, I always like to think of *Bed and*

Butter as my prentice piece. I was dreadfully immature when I wrote it.'

'I suppose you have that incredible effect of multiple orgasms on all your women readers?'

Auberon tugged his ear thoughtfully. 'Difficult to tell, I suppose. One can't really ask, when addressing ladies' literary luncheon clubs.'

'I get every one of your books the very day they come out.'

'From the library?'

'Of course not. I cherish them. I go down to Smith's and buy them.'

Auberon patted her soft, long-fingered hand. 'That's my girl.'

'But I expect I'm being dreadfully boring,' she apologized. 'You must get so much praise from your readers.'

'But never enough. I mean, *informed* appreciation.'

'That chapter in *The Mechanical Womb*.' She shut her eyes again. 'When the boy rapes the girl in the cornfield after he has decapitated his mother. Quite brilliant.'

'Yes, that scene did work rather well.'

Opening her eyes, she clutched his hand fiercely. 'And in *The Phallic Cymbal*, when the whole village goes mad with rabies . . . the broad canvas, the action, the detail . . . pure Tolstoy!'

'Need we bother about Tolstoy?' breathed Auberon, gazing at her steadily while returning the pressure of her fingers and brushing aside the intrusive flat leaves of a Swiss Cheese Plant with his free hand.

'Your famous silences! Chapter after chapter, with the characters saying absolutely nothing to each other.'

'Yes, the critics do rather like my silences.'

'Tell me, do you wait for inspiration or sit down at regular times?'

'Regular times. And I use a typewriter, not a pencil. Those are the two things everyone wants to know. But of course, a lot depends on being in the right atmosphere . . .' He drew closer. 'And the right people.'

'I do so desperately hope I shall have a chance to know you better while you're staying at the dean's.'

Auberon got even nearer. 'Can't we arrange something?'

The door opened. 'Have you met my husband?'

Auberon jerked round. Stepping briskly into the room was a tall middle-aged man with wispy gingery hair. His two features first to strike Auberon were enormous hands and restless green eyes with a wild flash to them. 'I was having a consultation with Dr M'Turk,' he explained hastily.

'I see.'

'Hamish, this is Auberon Dougal. You know, the writer.'

'I see.'

Auberon realized he was still clutching his psychiatrist's hand. He tore away. 'I was just demonstrating my mother fixation in childhood.'

'I see.'

'Mr Dougal is staying with the dean, Hamish.'

'I see.'

The conversation stopped.

The husband brushed aside a Sweetheart Plant extruding from a bamboo frame, then stood with legs apart and hands clasped behind his back in front of the fireplace, which contained a luxuriant Busy Lizzie. 'And how is that mean-minded little fusspot?'

'You mean me?' asked Auberon feebly.

'The dean. If I was in the remotest way responsible for the building which now ruins the view of not only our back garden but of half London, I should invite to perform the opening ceremony some other juvenile who suffered an incurable itch for vandalism. But it's not my affair, I suppose. I am, thank God, not a St Swithin's man. I operate at the Soho Clinic.'

'You're a psychiatrist, too?' Auberon tried shifting as far from his companion as the wickerwork permitted.

'No.' The man glared at him fiercely. 'Maggie here is the psychiatrist. She too practises at the Soho Clinic, as well as St Swithin's. There we are a team. Aren't we, my dear? I am a surgeon. A sex surgeon.' He produced his right hand from behind his back and rapidly flexed the fingers. 'I operate on people's glands, on people's brains. I change people's characters.'

'That must be extremely interesting,' suggested Auberon, staring back uncomfortably.

'Yes, It is. In these hands I have the power to influence not only men's thoughts, but their *very way of thinking*. Much more decisively, much more consistently, than all the great philosophers and orators in history.'

'*Most* interesting.'

'Maggie and I are doing some particularly rewarding work this moment on sex offenders. Aren't we, Maggie my love? Men who suffer from overpowerful sexual urges, you know. Men constantly in trouble with the police from interfering with women. You must know the familiar story, Mr Dougal? The man, seemingly respectable, who tricks his way into the house in the absence of the husband, then attempts to rape the unfortunate housewife on the sofa in her own front parlour.'

'I think I may have read about it occasionally in the papers,' said Auberon faintly.

Hamish M'Turk's eyes blazed even more. 'I'm

sure you have. These men . . . these monsters . . . what thought do they spare for the poor suffering woman? Or the poor suffering huband? Eh? Would *you* like to go through life constantly reminded that *your* dear wife had been violated by some coarse stranger?'

'I haven't really thought about it. But I should imagine it could be very awkward.'

There was another silence. The surgeon leant forward. 'The rapist I treat rapes but once,' he continued quietly. 'A little nick with the knife . . . and he is as peaceful as a castrated bull. More so. Thoughts of sex never enter his brain again. Never! You must write a book about this one day, Mr Dougal.'

'I really must.'

Hamish M'Turk straightened up. 'Now I expect the dean will be waiting for you at dinner. He is obsessively punctual in his habits. My wife reads your books, Mr Dougal. I regret that I am quite unable to. Though I do assure you that I have tried. Very hard. Maggie, show our visitor out.'

As she opened the sitting-room door, Dr Maggie M'Turk whispered under cover of an effervescent pot of Mind-Your-Own-Business, 'My clinic at St Swithin's. Two-thirty Monday afternoon.'

Auberon nodded. 'See you on the couch.'

10

It was Black Sunday for the dean.

His dark suit and formal collar seemed somehow uncomfortable outside the working week. But the chapel came as a surprise. There were flowers everywhere, arranged lovingly by the League of Friends of St Swithin's. The strong sun brought a garish light from the rich purples, crimsons and aquamarines of the saints in the windows. And the place was full. This puzzled him. He recognized a handful of students from the Christian Union – depressingly serious young men, he often thought, though setting a valuable example to the medical school in the way of haircuts, sobriety, and unwavering respect for the dean. The rest were females, mostly nurses in uniform. All the matron's charges seemed suddenly to have got religion. It was odd.

For most of the service the dean occupied himself pleasantly with mentally digging and replanting his garden. Then he sang all the way through 'Fight the Good Fight' to the wrong tune. Next, they sat. The Reverend Thomas Becket took for the first time the tubsized pulpit. The dean had expected him in his anorak and undervest, but wearing canonicals his lean frame, sallow bearded face and large eyes took a strikingly handsome look. Even his Cockneyfied voice had a new resonance and authority.

'In the three short days I have been in St Swithin's, my brothers and sisters, I have been able to reach my own diagnosis,' he began. 'The hospital is sick. Sick in its heart. Sick because it has forgotten the very reason for its existence – to show mercy towards the ill, to relieve pain and suffering, to succour the poor, to alleviate hardship and want, and to extend charity to all who are forced in their misery to enter our doors.'

'Most impressive,' murmured Josephine. 'Just look at Faith.'

The dean saw his daughter staring open-mouthed. He grunted.

'Of course, St Swithin's is full of scientific wonders, of which I would not presume to understand the workings. But is cold science all we have to offer, my brothers and sisters? Emphatically no!' The Reverend Becket slapped the rim of the pulpit. 'Compassion is still as valuable as any drug. In many cases, I should say *more* effective. And that in St Swithin's is sadly lacking.'

'What's that, dear?' hissed Josephine.

'Nothing,' muttered the dean angrily. 'I'd like to see this fellow use faith, hope and charity to cure even a case of simple rheumatism. I should prefer physiotherapy, heat and corticosteroids.'

'And what, my brothers and sisters, of the self-chosen instruments of mercy at St Swithin's? The doctors. For them, I have a simple message. "Physician, heal thyself." Luke four, twenty-three. What sickness is there! What indifference to man's spiritual needs! What self-importance! What arrogance! What cold detachment, what lack of love for their own brothers and sisters temporarily laid low!'

'Lionel!' Josephine gripped the dean's sleeve 'You can't creep out now,' she whispered urgently. 'You should have gone before we came.'

'It's not my bloody prostate,' he hissed back. 'I refuse to listen to further insults, however pious.'

'Sssh! Anyway, I agree with every word he says.'

The dean folded his arms and spent the rest of the sermon glaring at the cover of his prayerbook. Then he dropped a fifty-pence piece into the collection in mistake for ten. Finally, the Reverend Becket came back to his house and drank his sherry, and there he was in his own dining-room carving the fellow a slice of his prime shoulder of lamb.

'I *did* find your sermon so inspiring,' said Josephine across the well-polished mahogany dining-table. There were four of them. The dean's only comfort had been Auberon's invitation to lunch with his American publisher at the Hilton Hotel. 'Didn't *you*, Faith?'

'It was super, mummy.'

'Old Mr Nosworthy was very kind-hearted, of course, Mr Becket. But his sermons did sometimes remind me of the Lady President's address to the local Conservative Women's Association.'

'I'm afraid the middle-class conception of the Deity dies hard, Lady Lychfield.' The chaplain was wearing his clerical collar, and a bottle-green velvet suit with gold fringes to the sleeves. 'A gentleman who went to a good public school, is a member of the best golf clubs and employs a reliable stockbroker.'

'I'm afraid you must find *us* quite appallingly bourgeois. Formal Sunday lunch and all.'

'Enough fat for you?' hissed the dean, slipping a plate in front of him.

'Lovely, thanks. I know people say I've a bit of a chip on my shoulder. But I just can't help it. It's my nature. Or perhaps it's my name?' He smiled. 'This "turbulent priest", this "upstart clerk". '

'Roast potato?' growled the dean.

'Smashing. Mind, I'm looking forward to seeing the Queen next Thursday. I was even hoping Sir Lionel might present me.' The chaplain hesitated. 'My old mum wouldn't half be proud.'

'Mint sauce?' the dean muttered.

'Ta. When I called on your Sultan yesterday evening, Sir Lionel, he asked me to remind you about introducing *him*. He seemed pretty cosy up there, I thought. Though I strongly disapprove of privileged treatment, just because you can pay for it. Immoral, isn't it, if you think of it? Life-saving medicine should come like the water and drains. Same rate for all.'

'British medicine happens to be one of our most flourishing invisible exports.' The dean pointed his carving-fork at the chaplain. 'A constant procession of millionaires from the Persian Gulf come over here and leave various parts of themselves behind. I only wish the Government would recognize the fact, and remunerate its hospital consultants accordingly.'

'I expect I'll find these things out as I run myself in,' the chaplain said easily. 'I hope you're coming along to out-patients' waiting hall at ten tomorrow morning, Sir Lionel?'

'Of course not. It's my round in the wards. Why should I, pray?'

'It's the inaugural meeting of PUS.'

The dean frowned, taking his place at the table.

'And what the hell's that? It sounds more like a concern of the surgical side.'

'Patients' Unity Society. I'm organizing patient power in the hospital.' The dean winced. 'I mean, even sick people have the basic democratic right of organized peaceful protest, haven't they?'

The dean glared harder. 'What you bloody well mean is, everyone these days feels they have the right to break any laws they happen to find inconvenient, and to chuck bricks at innocent policemen with far less provocation than would incite me to write even a mildly phrased letter to *The Times*. That's it, isn't it? I realize that you are perfectly sincere, Mr Becket. But you are also perfectly naïve. You do not seem to have worked out a very simple calculation – that if we all exercised such rights as we enjoy, civilization would come to a halt in chaos tomorrow morning.'

The chaplain looked suddenly downcast.

'Sorry, Sir Lionel. I didn't mean to upset anyone. I thought I might have a bit of cooperation from you, that's all,' he said in a humble voice.

'And I from you,' the dean told him severely.

There was a silence. Josephine looked embarrassed. 'There's bread-and-butter pudding to follow,' she said brightly.

'I'm doing my best,' the Reverend Becket continued miserably. 'I know I put my foot in things. I know I've got this brash manner. I can't help it. I didn't want to be a hospital chaplain, you see.' He seemed to collapse suddenly in the full sternness of the dean's gaze. 'But the bishop sent me, because Mrs Dougal was bothering him so much. I wanted to be chaplain to a prison. Society there is much more easy for a simple chap like myself to cope with.'

'He'll have to resign,' said the dean, as the chaplain later left the house. 'Can't have a fellow like him at St Swithin's.'

'Lionel, you are cruel,' said Josephine. 'He's a little inexperienced, that's all.'

'I dislike to see amateurishness in any department of the hospital. And the way he's carrying on, we soon shan't be able to stick a needle in anyone without inciting a demonstration. It's all very well for him to blather on about charity and compassion, and all those lovely things. But the only job people thank us for is making them better, not telling them we're terribly sorry they're ill.'

'You *can't* get rid of him, anyway. He's not one of your awkward students, you know.'

'Can't I?' The dean paused in thought. 'Sir Lancelot was always trying to get rid of the last chaplain. He objected to old Nosworthy's insistence that he had right of access to the consultants' loo.'

'Well, Lancelot didn't succeed, did he?'

'I don't know . . . there was something Lancelot knew about Nosworthy. Something the rest of us didn't. It was all very strange. Perhaps he was blackmailing the poor old man? I wouldn't put it past Lancelot.' The dean stood scratching his chin as Josephine disappeared from the hall to the kitchen. Perhaps he should send the surgeon another cable on the subject? he wondered. But the damn fellow never seemed to respond. He might even be obliged to dispatch it reply paid.

That evening before dinner, Sir Lancelot Spratt sat in his white dinner-jacket at the ship's cocktail bar. On the counter before him was a malt whisky. On a stool at his side was Dulcie Yarborough.

'Hasn't anyone told you what lovely hands you've got, Lancelot?'

He looked down at his spread fingers. 'I have never been inclined to submit myself to lady manicurists.'

'I mean how powerful, how positive,' She stroked one with her finger tips. 'You could have been some great surgeon.'

'Unfortunately, I am unable adequately even to fillet a fried sole.'

II

At nine sharp on Monday morning the dean came through the self-opening glass doors of St Swithin's, rubbing his hands at the prospect of not only an energetic but an exciting week ahead. He collided with Professor Oliphant in a white coat, arms stretched out stiffly at an angle of forty-five degrees from his sides.

'Good God, Gerry, have you got some sort of orthopaedic condition?'

'My white coat, dean, has been starched by the hospital laundry. Which doubtless contains the very latest mechanisms of ablutionary science, but necessitates getting my hands into the sleeves with a hammer and crowbar.'

'I'll speak to the laundry superintendent.' The dean tried to push past, but the professor's well starched sleeve stopped him. 'The new operating theatre trolleys, dean. Did you know that they won't fit into the lifts, however ingeniously we turn them? So the patients have to be decanted on to the old ones. Possibly they are too doped with premedication to care, but it adds to the noticeable atmosphere in St Swithin's of utter and ineradicable confusion.'

'Only in the eyes of uninitiated observers,' countered the dean, still trying to get past.

'Precisely. Which category includes all our patients. God knows why they don't run out in panic. By the way, there arrived in my house at seven o'clock this morning an Italian orthopaedic surgeon, from whose appearance

'What a shame. Or perhaps some wonderful concert pianist? Holding your audience in thrall.'

'I regret that I never progressed at the pianoforte beyond "Chopsticks". And I was given to understand by my elders that I was particularly inept at that.'

Dulcie continued stroking the back of his smooth, pale, freckled fist. 'I wonder how many women have felt their delicate caress?' she asked dreamily.

'Sadly, the lightest touch brought my poor late wife out in a rash for weeks. She was, according to our family doctor, highly allergic.' He was aware of a steward with a silver salver beside him.

'Cable, sir.'

'Throw it over the side.'

'The reply has already been paid for, sir.'

'Please keep it as a tip.'

'Very good, sir.'

'Those hands of yours,' murmured Dulcie. 'You know, they have a quite hypnotic effect on me. I wonder where they've been.'

'You'd be surprised,' said Sir Lancelot.

and melodious voice I expect at any moment to break into an aria about slipped discs. Also a rather surly gynaecologist from Belgium.'

'Good. I can speak French to him.'

'You can't. He's not a Walloon, and insists on sticking to Flemish.'

'You really must excuse me,' persevered the dean, making another effort to pass. 'I am going to hold a rehearsal.'

'You're not. Do you know where I spent most of Sunday?'

The dean sighed. 'The lift?'

Professor Oliphant nodded. 'How did you guess? You are coming to the roof to inspect the mechanism for yourself.'

'I assure you that I am a complete duffer at mechanical devices. I nearly electrocute myself at home whenever I change a fuse.'

'You'll learn. Come along. You'd better wear a white coat, too. It is all appallingly greasy.'

The professor spiked him with his glance. The dean knew from miserable experience there was no escape. 'I'll have to tell the Queen and Duke to clear off.' Professor Oliphant raised his eyebrows. 'I mean my daughter and my house-physician. They are understudies, as is said on the boards.'

He made a dismissive gesture to the pair sitting on a bench against the wall, and allowed the professor to steer him into the lift.

'But I don't see why we can't just go down to the local registry office and get married on one of my afternoons off,' Clem Undercroft continued his conversation with Faith. 'I'm sure it's quite easy to arrange. People are getting married all the time, six days a week. It must be easier than getting delivery of a new car. And your father needn't even know until I've shot my bolt, as it were.'

'No, Clem, no.' Faith's eyes were half shut, her mouth was open and she was breathing heavily. 'Don't tempt me, *please* don't tempt me. It's tearing me apart inside.'

'Come to that, why should your father object, and who cares anyway?' He sounded more petulant than defiant. 'He's a miserable old sod. If he had his own way, nobody would ever get married or have any sort of fun at all.'

She squeezed his hand, hidden between them as they sat close on the bench. 'It's not that, Clem. It's something else.'

'Don't say you're too young?' Faith felt he looked very satisfyingly miserable, particularly with his glasses more awry than usual. 'Why, at seventeen these days you're a mature woman. You could have a bouncing baby already, and still have kept it legal. Of course, I'm only provisionally registered,' he admitted. 'I'm not allowed to use the doctors' car park or sign people up for cremations, and that sort of thing. And your old man has to give me a certificate at the end of my six months, saying I've performed my duties to his satisfaction.' Clem's face suddenly fell further. 'Christ, I'd forgotten that. Your father refused to sign up one of his housemen because he pinched his umbrella on a wet afternoon.'

'Oh, Clem,' Faith breathed. 'How you must be suffering for me.'

'I am. And it's getting me down. I wanted you since the moment I saw you. When we were being the Queen and the Duke. Thank God your father had that row with old Ollie, or we'd never have got acquainted properly out in the car park.'

'But Clem, it is not to be.'

'Why not, for God's sake?' He paused, adjusting his glasses. 'If you don't want to marry me, won't you at least let me take you out for a Chinese nosh one evening?'

Faith turned her gaze on him solemnly. 'I *do* understand your problem, Clem.'

'I know. I lack charm.'

'You want to possess my body.'

'Well, to tell the truth, I wouldn't mind,' he agreed.

'All men are the same. They want to possess my body. I have another.'

He looked mystified. 'Another body?'

'No. Another man.'

'Not one of those coarse little randy students – '

'No, Clem. He is an older person. Mature. Sophisticated and cultured. Witty and famous.'

'Go on?' exclaimed Clem.

'The world-famous author, Auberon Dougal.'

'Never heard of him.'

'He writes wonderful books. Last Saturday morning he tried to rape me.'

Clem looked aghast.

'I fought him off. Though I think he will try again. I'm afraid he is rather a chronic rapist.'

They fell silent. 'Won't you come up to my room in the residents' quarters?' Clem suggested faintly. 'I've got some super records. I promise not to rape you. Or the opposite, if you'd prefer.'

'I shall have to consider very seriously whether I give myself to you, Clem. But I'll come and hear your super records. How about next Thursday about twelve midday?'

'But that's great!' He stopped. 'Wait a minute.

Twelve o'clock next Thursday – that's only half an hour before the Queen's arriving.'

'I know. For once I shall be absolutely certain of having dear daddy definitely right out of the way. See you.'

With tripping step she made for the automatic doors.

In the study of the dean's house in Lazar Row, Auberon Dougal ripped a page from the typewriter and started again.

Page I

THE TRUTH ABOUT HORTENSE

Chapter One

That late afternoon in August, as the woman doctor made her way through the fields to the poet dying of tubercoolosis she felt the sharp tang, which warns how near approach the narrow days of winter. 'Yet mankind,' she thought, 'has not yet tired of the God-given days of summer.' The sun was a burning sovereign in the sky, but already in the valleys autumnal mists twined, smoke-like.

He turned with a smile. 'Hello, Faith. Come in. Writing novels would be absolutely intolerable if it weren't for the interruptions.'

'Uncle, can I ask you something about the fundamental truths of life?'

'How wise, to pick precisely the right person.'

'I feel you're the only one in this whole house I can really *talk* to, uncle.'

'I'm sure you're absolutely correct. Your parents are beginning to strike me as very odd indeed, since my last visit. They're ageing, I suppose. Had you noticed how they keep looking at me round corners? And when your father found me rummaging for an aspirin in his bathroom cabinet, he kept following me about with a quite obscene length of red rubber tubing and a funnel.

I don't look ill, do I? I don't think I've ever felt better, since leaving Samantha.'

'That's what I wanted to ask about. Marriage.'

'You're contemplating it?'

'I have had an offer,' Faith replied solemnly.

'Then go ahead. At your age, marriage is a wonderful bit of fun which shouldn't be missed. Maybe one day when Samantha and I are divorced, even I shall get married again.' He looked dreamily at the ceiling, his imagination busy. 'A new girl. New cooking. New habits. New conversation. New arguments. New underwear scattered about the bedroom. Though I suppose these days most women's underwear is exactly the same.'

'He wishes me to indulge in premarital intercourse.'

'Now you sound like Samantha. She wanted to stamp it out, you know. She used to sound as though it were some sort of insect.'

'But you know that my father has very high moral views.'

Auberon gave a loud laugh. 'Listen, dearie – I'd never breathe a word of this to your mother, but do you know that last Thursday night, when you were tucked up in your virtuous little bed, your father was on the prowl round the most sordid corners of Soho? Samantha saw him. It was one of the last things she ever told me. Of course, your old man tried to pretend he was just inspecting the depravity as a matter of painful duty. Everyone does. Samantha believed him. I certainly wouldn't. I don't want to wound your feelings, but the old pill-roller's a bit of a hypocrite.'

She smiled gently. 'Thank you, uncle. It is a relief to feel freed from my filial obligations. They were becoming a bit painful.'

He turned back to the typewriter. 'To work. I've got to leave in an hour for lunch with a magazine owner at the Mirabelle Restaurant. I must write *something*,' he added desperately. 'Even to earn no more than the scorn of my critics.'

'I don't see why you can't turn and attack your critics, uncle.'

'According to the highly professional novelist Anthony Trollope,' he told her, ' "No one thinks of defending himself to a newspaper except an ass. You may write what's as true as the gospel, but they'll know how to make fun of it." You see? And Fleet Street hasn't changed since his day.'

'I think even to write a book at all is a wonderful achievement,' Faith said admiringly.

'How kind.'

She was looking over his shoulder. 'It's spelt t-u-b-e-r-c-u-l-o-s-i-s, and that "which" clause shouldn't have a comma in front of it.'

'I'm obliged,' said Auberon. 'And I might add that I have a great sadness for those who can do nothing with the English language except spell it correctly.'

12

AT two twenty five that afternoon Auberon Dougal arrived at St Swithin's in a taxi from the Mirabelle Restaurant in Mayfair, walked quickly through the self-opening doors, and turned to search through a directory of hospital departments on one of the marble walls. Psychiatry was on the thirtieth floor. He took the lift to the top of the building. As he stepped out he saw the name DR M. M'TURK painted on the door immediately opposite. He knocked and went in.

'Ah! My patient.' Dr M'Turk rose to greet him, hands fluttering. She wore a brown suede trouser suit with leather fringes at all free edges, her fair hair now held in place by a knotted thong of horse-whip. The room itself, Auberon saw with approval, was light and cheerful, and still smelt of fresh paint. The psychiatrist was standing behind a small, modern desk with a half-sized bust in pink marble of a man with a beard, whom he took to be Freud. She indicated a comfortable looking couch with a dark red cover along one wall. Auberon sat down.

'There's one thing I'd better confess from the start, Dr M'Turk.'

She settled herself close to him. 'Maggie, please. I always use christian names. So essential for establishing rapport.'

'What's rapport?'

'Breaking the glass which lies between us.' She made polishing motions with the flat of her hand. 'Succeeding in that constant attempt of every human to understand another one – which so often and so miserably fails.'

He thought this might be worth putting in his next book. 'Well, Maggie, I'm an awful fraud.'

She looked at him curiously. 'Are you tortured with feelings of guilt?'

'Frankly, I *am* a little,' he admitted cheerfully. 'You see, there's nothing the matter with me. Nothing whatever. Physically, mentally or spiritually. I didn't really come round to your place last Saturday with the idea of getting a medical consultation. I came with the idea of getting some material for a novel. Since then I've been feeling rather ashamed of myself. So I decided that I really ought to confess. I do hope you're not too cross with me?'

She softly stroked his brow. 'You poor, poor sick child.'

Auberon edged away slightly. 'But honestly, I feel fine. In terrific form. You see, I've just left my wife. She's Mrs Samantha Dougal, whom you must have seen on the box.'

Dr M'Turk nodded. 'I only hope she's a phoney. She'd be inexcusable if she were sincere.'

'Well, a bit of both, perhaps. She is what you'd call an exhibitionist. And she's one of those incorrigible people who Virginia Woolf described as dabbling their fingers self-approvingly in the stuff of others' souls. But enough of Samantha. Now we've separated, I'm eating like a horse, sleeping like a top, and enjoying the most delightfully pornographic dreams.'

'You're not well, Auberon,' Dr M'Turk went on stroking his forehead, her pale smooth face close to his, her blue eyes striking him as wide as a cat's in the dark. 'You are sick, sick, sick.'

He looked alarmed. 'Go on?'

'You are so pitiably in need of my care.'

'Am I?'

'You are really quite desperately neurotic,' she explained gently. 'Like all great artists. Beethoven, Proust, van Gogh.' Auberon looked more cheerful. 'The very act of creation is in itself a psychopathic symptom, naturally. It indicates a violently unstable personality underneath. Beethoven was totally anti-social. That's why there are so many houses dedicated to his memory in Vienna. He kept having to move. And van Gogh had this tendency to cut off his ears. You, Auberon, are a typical hysteric.'

'But I don't think I've ever had an attack of hysterics in my life.' He sounded uneasy.

'In psychiatry the word "hysteric" has a special meaning,' she continued softly. 'It refers to those whose emotions – though often violent and dramatically expressed – are but showers and sunlight on the surface of the ocean, leaving the depths untouched.'

Auberon scratched his ear. 'I suppose . . . yes, I suppose if I think back a bit, to my rows with Samantha, for instance, I could say just that.'

'Did you wet the bed much as a child?'

'Not awfully, I think.'

'Are you a hypochondriac? Like Carlyle with his guts?'

'Living with Lionel Lychfield it's difficult to be anything else. He comes home and talks about ghastly diseases as though they were the flowers in his garden.'

'But *are* you a hypochondriac?' She came even nearer. 'Think.'

'I'm of a delicate constitution, certainly. Yes, perhaps you're right.'

'Are you the tidy sort?'

'Now, it's funny you should ask that. Samantha was always complaining I insisted on keeping absolutely everything exactly in place, all round the house. She of course is a domestic litter lout.'

'Ah! You're obsessional.'

'Am I?'

'You're stuck in the anal stage.'

'That does sound rather uncomfortable.'

'You get depressed?'

'At times.'

'And elated?'

'At others.'

'You worry?'

'I certainly am worrying now.'

'My poor Auberon. I'm afraid I must tell you that you are a hypochondriac hysteric manic-depressive anxiety-neurotic anally-fixated post-enuretic psychopath.'

'Oh, my God.' He covered his face with his hands. 'But I'd no idea I was in such a mess. When I walked in here I was perfectly happy, right on top of the world.'

'Thank God you came to me in time. You just *thought* you felt completely well, that's all. Psychologically, you're a whited sepulchre. All nasty inside.'

He grasped her hand with both his. 'But you can cure me?'

'Yes.' Her head jerked back. 'I can.'

'Oh, thank God!'

'If you put absolute faith in me.'

'Absolute, I promise.' He hesitated. 'How long will it take?'

'Years. Perhaps several.'

Auberon felt this a not unpleasant prospect. 'What do I have to do?'

She stood up with an expansive gesture. 'For a start, lie down on the couch. Relax.'

'But how can I possibly relax when I've just learned that inside I'm as twisted as a bowl of spaghetti?'

She leant close to him, stroking his cheek. 'You must *try*, Auberon. Or I shall have to draw the blinds and hypnotize you.'

'That sounds quite nice.'

'You think so?' She stayed looking piercingly at him. Then she broke away in the direction of the desk, continuing in a businesslike voice, 'I'm sure you're going to be one of my most interesting cases.'

'Do I accept that as a compliment or a warning?'

'You'll make an excellent subject for psychoanalysis. You are extraordinarily suggestible, and will respond most satisfyingly to my commands.'

'Will I?'

'Lie down, please.'

He threw himself flat.

'There. What did I say?' She clicked down her ballpoint, sitting beside the pink marble bust of Freud and starting to write in a blue folder which Auberon noticed was marked NOT TO BE GIVEN TO THE PATIENT. 'Let's begin. The psychological history. Childhood. Did you suffer from tantrums, nail-biting, stammering, night terrors, fear of closed spaces, fear of open spaces, fear of the dark, somnambulism, stammering, school phobia, convulsions?'

'Frequently.'

She made a note. 'Now, occupation. How many jobs?'

'Before my first book was published, I followed almost

all manual occupations from cement-mixer to casino croupier.'

'A poor work-record. Tut. Home background. Any incest?'

'No. We were terribly bad at all family games.'

She wrote another line. 'Sexual practice and inclinations. Masturbation, homosexuality, heterosexual experiences? Inside, before and outside marriage? And does it worry you?'

'Have you noticed that little habit you've got? Your hands hover over your papers like a pair of humming birds while you decide what to say next.'

'Really?' She inspected her fingers.

Auberon propped himself on his elbow. 'And did you know you have one of those exciting broad mouths, which indicate sensuality in a woman.'

'They don't.'

'Well, men imagine they do. Which is the same thing, isn't it? You know, it's odd. But I've never imagined a psychiatrist could ever be a female.'

'You're not anti-women's lib, I hope?' she asked sharply.

'On the contrary, I like women. Women as people, if it's remotely possible to think of them that way. They're non-aggressive, always eager to please, and will do anything for a man if he's sufficiently nice to them or treats them badly enough.'

'And they take the faintest professional criticism as a personal insult,' she added.

'Exactly. Like my wife Samantha.'

Dr M'Turk put down her ballpoint. 'Auberon, I have already decided what treatment to prescribe for you. It's really quite obvious. I think I can get much better results with it, much more quickly than with established methods.'

'Nothing dangerous, I hope?' he asked quickly.

'Oh, no. Not at all.'

'I don't really want to be a guinea-pig for something not tried out on people properly.'

'This has been tried out on people for a very considerable time.'

She stood up, crossing the room thoughtfully, hands pressed together. 'I suppose you've heard about a form of psychotherapy – it's practised in America – generally called "the love treatment"?'

Auberon sat up abruptly. 'You mean the psychiatrist and the patient sort of go to couch together?'

'Exactly. It is of course just one form of therapy available, among many. One could give electric shocks instead. But the treatment has its uses in certain cases – which, naturally, must be picked purely on the psychiatrist's objective scientific judgement.'

'Which requires considerable professional skill,' he agreed quickly.

'I should like to think so. I have been able to form a diagnosis, Auberon, which tells me that in your particular case such therapy would be *most* valuable. It goes without saying, you will regard it as a perfectly proper and virtuous activity. It is therapy, not enjoyment. Look upon it like taking a daily dose of medicine.'

'Daily?' Auberon had his jacket half off. 'Maggie, I assure you of my fullest co-operation – '

She was on the couch, hands trembling against him. 'Oh, Auberon. I want to give myself to you. In the interests of science, naturally, but I do so want to give myself.'

'Maggie, I – ' He stopped. 'What about your husband? Him with the nifty little operations? Does he share your views on treatment?'

'Hamish and I have no time for petty little bourgeois

jealousies,' she continued breathlessly. 'They simply perpetuate the family unit, which as everyone knows is the prison-house of the soul.' She stopped him taking his jacket off completely with a fluttering hand. 'No, no. Not now. A nurse, anyone, could blunder in at any minute.'

'When then?' he asked eagerly.

'Come up here on Thursday, about noon.'

'I'll be waiting . . .' He frowned. 'That's funny. I imagined something was happening next Thursday around noon. Oh, yes, the dean and his royal official opening.'

'Exactly.' She clasped her hands excitedly. 'All the clinics are cancelled and everyone will be intensely occupied with the festivities. We can be sure of remaining absolutely undisturbed.'

'Great. You *are* a clever woman, you know.'

'From you, Auberon, that is flattery indeed.'

'Yes, but what about all those neuroses and phobias and things you said I'd got wrong with me?' he recalled.

'Oh, everybody has those,' she said lightly. 'It's only since the invention of psychiatry that a little madness in human beings has been thought at all abnormal.'

13

'I DON'T suppose *you* know any amusing stories?' the dean asked his wife gloomily as he entered their sitting-room at six-thirty that Monday evening. 'It's getting quite desperate. Surely they must tell funny stories on the committee of the League of Friends?'

'I'm afraid we take ourselves rather seriously, dear.'

The front door slammed behind him in the hallway. 'Who's that?' he asked irritably.

'Auberon. He's dining with a film producer at Les Ambassadeurs.'

The dean unlocked the corner cupboard. 'How much longer is the fellow staying here? Surely he must go back to Samantha in Guildford, if only to collect his laundry? I'm fed up with him wearing all my things. If he *does* kill himself, he might at least do it in his own underpants.'

'It's remarkable how your clothes fit him, dear. Considering Auberon looks so much more robust than you do.'

The dean snorted, pouring two glasses of sherry. 'I've never understood how Samantha managed to put up with a vacuous slacker like him as long as she did. Particularly when she expresses so often the robust Victorian virtues of hard work, thrift and carbolic soap.'

'You never mentioned you saw Samantha while you were marauding all alone round the strip joints of Soho, after the rugger club dinner last Thursday night.'

The dean spilt his sherry. 'Who told you that?'

'I have my sources of information.'

'I had to show I was a good sport, that's all.'

'Like the time when you were a houseman at St Swithin's, and rang the nurses' home fire alarm so you could rescue them in their nighties with ladders from the windows?'

The dean coloured. 'Anyway, the performance last Thursday was extremely boring. To a man like myself, who has seen more naked flesh than Samantha or Lord What's-is-name have had hot dinners. Besides, I was with Lancelot. He insisted we left early, before the two girls in the bath really got interesting.'

Josephine laughed. 'It's always nice to have confirmed that your husband is a perfectly normal man like any other.' The telephone rang. 'I'll answer it. It's probably the League of Friends.'

The dean poured himself another sherry. He sat in his armchair, sipping slowly, listening to his wife's indistinct voice in the hallway and wondering which viper in his well-bitten bosom had split on him. He had suffered another strenuous day, but now he could relax for the evening – a good dinner, perhaps a little Mozart, a glance through the *Lancet*. He looked at his watch. He wondered what time that strip show started. It could be curious to see what those girls did in the bath.

Josephine came back. 'Who was it?' he asked.

'Samantha.'

'Oh. Wanted Auberon, I take it?'

'No. She didn't even want Auberon to know she'd telephoned.'

'Where is she? In Guildford, doubtless?'

'She's in jail.'

'Well, I suppose she can't be expected to stay at home

all week . . .' The dean jumped up. '*Where* did you say?'

'In jail. To be more exact, in the cells at Curzon Street police station.'

'How in God's name did she get there?'

'By shoplifting and assaulting a policeman.'

'She must be mad. Mad. If this gets in the papers, it'll be terrible for her. Absolutely ruin her income.'

'But it most certainly *will* be in the papers, Lionel. Getting arrested is just one of the things you can't do discreetly.'

The dean put his hands behind his back, pacing the carpet anxiously. 'I can just see tomorrow's headlines – "Mrs Samantha Dougal on Theft and Violence Charge". Quite grotesque. Like seeing the Archbishop of Canterbury leading in the winner of the Derby. What shop was it? What did she lift?'

'Plushroses in Piccadilly. She took a small pot of caviar and a pair of see-through knickers.'

The dean winced. 'It wouldn't have looked so bad if she'd pinched something wholesome, like a spade from the gardening department. Or even one of her husband's books.'

'You must go to Curzon Street straight away, Lionel.'

'But I'm just going to have my dinner.'

'Of course you're not. You don't intend to leave the Chairman of the League of Friends of St Swithin's to spend the night on a straw palliasse, do you?'

'Can't she bail herself out, like the students after their rugger dinners?'

'No. Apparently the policeman she assaulted is in quite a state. At first they thought he was the victim of a gang.'

'Then what can *I* do? They won't let her out just because I ask nicely.'

'They might if you say you're her doctor. Tell them she's ill.'

'But she isn't.'

'Of course she is. Samantha would never have done anything like this if she were normal. Anyway, she sounded quite hysterical on the phone.'

'Oh, all right, all right,' the dean agreed reluctantly. 'Though why can't Auberon take responsibility?' he complained. 'His proper place is at her side in the cell, instead of continually gorging himself in expensive restaurants.'

He took his black homburg and reversed his new Rolls from his garage across the road. He performed as he did so a familiar little psychological somersault. He tried to convince himself once again that he had no particular affection for his sister-in-law.

Or rather, he told himself as he drove out of Lazar Row, he had an entirely *cerebral* fondness for her. He simply loved her intellect. Her fiery spirit. Her superb organizing ability. Her flair for communication and for human relations. And of course her moral courage, the dean reflected as he turned towards the West End. He certainly wouldn't have exposed himself to icy blasts of ridicule and the shrivelling sunshine of contempt with the abandon of Mrs Samantha Dougal. For principles in which she believed and others didn't – or, as she complained bitterly, were inanely indifferent to. A paragon among women.

Approaching Regent's Park the dean let his mind stray further into a regular pleasant little fantasy. Supposing he had married Mrs Samantha Dougal rather than Josephine? Samantha was a trifle plump, of course, but like many skinny men he had a fondness for well-covered women. He felt this was motivated by Darwinian principles of natural selection. Admittedly,

Josephine was the better cook. And if he *hadn't* married Josephine in the first place, he would never have met his sister-in-law anyway. He sighed gently, regretting sadly that monogamy and the office of the dean of St Swithin's were synonymous.

He crossed Berkeley Square and parked his car outside the police station, hurrying up the steps between posters exhorting the public to take out licences for their television sets and keep a sharp look-out for the Colorado beetle. Inside was a counter, behind which sat a red-faced sergeant in his shirt sleeves.

'Good evening. I am a doctor.'

'Evening, doctor. Had your drugs pinched?'

'I am here on an extremely serious matter. I gather you are holding in custody Mrs Samantha Dougal?'

'I'll say!' A broad grin lit the sergeant's face. A shirt-sleeved constable entering the room at the same time gave a guffaw. 'Patient of yours, doctor?'

'In this instance, yes.' The dean eyed the two policemen severely. It did not seem to him at all a laughing matter. He realized what the patients felt at St Swithin's, lying naked on a chilly couch and wondering what awful disease they had got, while the houseman gaily chatted up a couple of nurses.

' "Mrs Morality", ' the sergeant quoted jovially. 'A real tearaway, she is.'

'I can hardly believe that,' said the dean stiffly.

'You ought to see the mess she made of the arresting officer's uniform.'

'You ought to see the mess she made of the officer,' grinned the constable.

'Luckily, doctor, he's not nearly as serious as he thought, according to the hospital. We can let her out. I think he was more scared than anything.'

'But how did this disaster happen?' demanded the

dean, puzzled. 'I've known Mrs Samantha Dougal for years. It's entirely out of character.'

'With women you never know. Do you, doctor? They're unpredictable. Like lions in the circus. Just when you think you've got them properly trained, they go and bite your head off.'

The dean was in no mood for philosophy. 'I have come to secure her release, and as quicky as possible. On medical grounds, she should never be locked up. She suffers from claustrophobia, very chronically.'

'But you've got to laugh, haven't you?' the sergeant continued amiably. 'Mrs Samantha Dougal in the nick. Though I reckon if you spend your life telling people to behave themselves, it doesn't do any harm finding yourself for once on the wrong side of the bars. Mind you, I enjoy her on Sundays on the telly. I like someone who speaks her mind. And . . .' He made motions in front of his shirt-pockets. 'Got a full house up in the balcony, hasn't she?'

The dean slapped his cheque book on the desk. 'If you will name the amount of bail – '

'Cash won't be necessary, doctor. Just a form to sign. It'll be Greek Street magistrates' court at ten o'clock tomorrow morning.'

Two minutes later, the shirt-sleeved policeman produced Mrs Samantha Dougal from somewhere down below.

'Samantha!'

'Lionel!'

She came through the flap in the counter. She looked pinker than usual. Her auburn hair still tumbled voluptuously round her shoulders. Her full lower lip trembled. From her glistening eyes dropped two tears – which the dean thought to be quite twice the size of anyone else's. A second later he had clasped her warm, soft, quivering body and she was sobbing on his shoulder, knocking his homburg askew.

'There, there,' The dean patted her. 'There, there, *there*. But whatever happened?'

'I don't know. I just don't know. I was so upset at Auberon leaving home, I suppose.'

'But isn't he always leaving home? Twice a year regularly, I gathered.'

'I know. But this time I felt it was for good. He took all his credit cards with him.' She pulled the handkerchief from the dean's top pocket and blew her nose. 'I'd come up to Town to record my show for next Sunday, and I wandered into Plushroses because I felt deep down I wanted something luxurious to console me. Then I must have had a complete mental lapse. When I was stopped by that woman detective outside, I just couldn't believe it. About what happened next, I'm confused. I must have gone berserk. Is the policeman expected to live?'

'Samantha,' explained the dean dramatically. 'I have come to take you away.'

'Oh, Lionel!'

She started shaking with sobs again, clutching him the more tightly. The dean patted her, adding a little stroke or two. 'Listen, Samantha. I've worked everything out. Ask Greek Street court tomorrow to remand you on bail for a month. Meanwhile I'll get the very best legal advice – from Mr Humphrey Fletcher-Boote, QC. He's an old schoolfriend who'd do anything for me. A tremendous expert on the criminal law, with which you have so unfortunately collided. In fact, they call him the Scarlet Pimpernel of the Old Bailey. If he'd been briefed by the Great Train Robbers, I understand they'd not only have got off but been allowed to keep the engine as a souvenir.'

'Oh, *Lionel*!'

'There, there, there, there, there, there, there, there, *there*.' The dean stroked her cheek, with an incidental little tickle to the lobe of her ear. He became suddenly aware of the two policemen looking at him curiously. He pushed Samantha away. 'This is a very sensitive patient of mine, sergeant. She has to be handled most sympathetically.'

The sergeant grinned again. 'Can I have your autograph, Mrs Dougal? The kids won't half be tickled when I tell them I've met you.'

'Give a bit more interest, like, to your show on Sunday,' added the constable. 'We were going to Southend, but now we'll stay at home and watch.'

'How irritating,' muttered the dean as he hurried Samantha outside. 'The police seemed to treat it as some sort of joke, when they were witnessing stark tragedy. Those men really do take a flippant attitude towards their work. I shall write a sharp letter to the Commissioner. Yes, officer, what is it?' he demanded, as another policeman approached from the kerb, grinning broadly.

'Have you been doing business in the station, sir?'

'Well, I have not driven all the way from north London to report a lost dog.'

'Sorry, sir, but I'm having to book you for parking. It's a double yellow line. You did it right outside the front door of the nick, too! You've got to laugh, haven't you?'

14

Before the dean was awake the following morning – the Tuesday, but two short days before the Queen's arrival – Sir Lancelot Spratt had already finished his breakfast. This was through the clocks aboard his cruise ship by then being advanced a couple of hours. Sir Lancelot had chosen a meal of Scots porridge with brown sugar and clotted Devon cream, stewed figs, a pair of kippers, eggs, bacon, kidney, sausages and grilled mushrooms, as an afterthought a small portion of kedgeree, a paw paw, toast with Oxford marmalade, and two pots of coffee. He sat in his T-shirt and khaki shorts inspecting the menu to see what he had been obliged to miss – the Bismarck herring, the Madras curry, the Aberdeen bloater, the eleven other varieties of egg, the passion fruit, the lamb cutlet, the muffins with Highland honey, the brain fritters, the American waffle, the hot chocolate, the York ham. . . .

'It's hardships suffered by ancient mariners, I suppose,' he murmured. 'Their diet of ship's biscuit, salt pork and scouse. Some atavistic memory obliges shipping companies to do themselves so well. Though God knows what effect it's having on my weight.' He made a mental note to try the bloater and curry the following morning. 'Steward!'

'Sir?'

Sir Lancelot inclined his head towards the empty chair at his table. 'Mrs Yarborough does not seem to be taking breakfast this morning.'

'No, sir. The lady is having a pot of tea in her cabin, as she is feeling poorly.'

'Poorly?' Sir Lancelot's eyebrows went up in a businesslike way. The weather was flat calm. It couldn't be seasickness. 'I suppose I'd better get down to her cabin and take a look at her.'

'Take a look, sir?' The steward regarded him curiously.

'I mean, I'd better look into her cabin some time. She might need a little company. Not of course that I am in the habit of entering ladies' sleeping apartments.'

'I'm sure you're not, sir. Would you care to finish off your breakfast with a devilled leg of partridge? The chef does them deliciously.'

'I think I am fuelled until the bouillon and biscuits at eleven.' Sir Lancelot rose from the table.

Two minutes later, he was tapping gently on the door of Dulcie's cabin. He found her sitting up in a black nightie, reading a book.

'Why, it's Lancelot! How terribly kind of you to call. I was getting awfully bored with the day already. Though I wish you'd given me the chance to make myself more presentable. I'm sure you must absolutely hate looking at people when they're ill.'

'On the contrary, Dulcie, I have done quite a deal of sick visiting in my time. Occasionally I get the sensation that I make a profession of it.'

She shut her book. 'I'm sure this is something quite trivial.'

'You do, indeed?' He stood stroking his beard. Bags under the eyes – indicative of dehydration. A slight flush. That meant a fever. In his experience, he'd put it from her appearance at a hundred point five degrees. Chest moving symmetrically, no cough. Therefore slight possibility of a respiratory infection. Now, the knees were interesting. They remained drawn up under the bed-clothes. Quite strongly indicative of abdominal dis-comfort. He started counting her pulse from the faint shimmer of the carotid artery in her neck.

'Lancelot, you *are* looking stern. From the way you're inspecting me, I might be one of your sick pigs.'

'Do forgive me,' he apologized hastily. 'I was just wondering exactly what your trouble was.'

She looked at him coyly. 'But I could hardly tell *you*, could I?'

'Of course you can. After all, I'm a . . .' He checked himself. 'A very sympathetic listener.'

'I'm sure you are. I've sent for the ship's doctor.'

'Good God. You haven't?'

She looked surprised. 'Why not? If I was at home, I'd send for my own doctor, wouldn't I?'

'Yes, but damn it, this ship's quack – '

'I know.' She wagged her finger. 'You're one of those tough men who don't believe in doctors. Aren't you? Well, in a way I agree with you. I think they often do far more harm than good, and they all scare you terribly. I fancy they do it on purpose. Just to impress you how terribly clever and powerful they are. Or at least, imagine they are. Personally, I could never bear to meet a doctor socially. They're real bogey men.'

'Some of my best friends are doctors,' he murmured.

'Really? Well, perhaps they can become quite human over a few drinks. I gather a lot of them are alcoholics. The ship's doctor will probably fix me up with a bottle of medicine. Though I hear from the other passengers his fees are quite outrageous. I suppose that's inescapable, as he enjoys a monopoly. There can't be another doctor for hundreds of miles in all directions.'

'I do not object to Dr Runchleigh's commercial outlook. That at least is highly effective, which is more than can be said for his professional abilities.'

'Lancelot, you're being perfectly nasty to the poor man. Everyone says he's terribly clever, as well as being so enormously charming.'

'Clever? He's an absolute bloody fool. He wouldn't know the difference between measles and malaria.'

She looked a little upset. 'How *can* you say cruel things like that?'

'Because I happen to be far better qualified . . . ' Sir Lancelot swallowed. He continued quietly, 'Because all patients are qualified to give opinions on their doctors.'

She laughed. 'You just took a dislike to him on sight, didn't you? I could tell that, when he introduced himself in the saloon yesterday.'

'Oh, I'm perfectly familiar with his sort. They keep trying to bamboozle me when I'm examining.'

'Examining what?'

'The situation,' said Sir Lancelot airily, as a knock came on the cabin door, followed by the silvery head of the ship's doctor himself.

'Good morning, Mrs Yarborough. A little off colour, are we?'

'Good morning, doctor. How very kind of you to call on me so quickly. I do hope that I didn't interrupt your breakfast?'

'We medical men, Mrs Yarborough, have to accustom ourselves to our meals being interrupted.' He came into the cabin, lips pursed in a knowing little smile. 'Our patients, of course, always come first. Particularly such charming ones as yourself, Mrs Yarborough, if I may say so.'

'But how nice.'

He nodded briefly at Sir Lancelot. 'I was expecting to see you in my surgery for treatment of your fits.'

'And you may continue to.'

Dr Runchleigh looked put out. 'Then I trust we are keeping well?'

'Why the hell shouldn't we be?'

'We must look after ourselves, mustn't we? Particularly at our age. These cool tropical nights, we never know when we might catch a chill.'

'We take care to tell our steward to shut our porthole, and keep draughts from the back of our blasted neck.'

Dr Runchleigh's finely-shaped nostrils quivered slightly. 'I now intend to examine Mrs Yarborough.'

'Go ahead,' invited Sir Lancelot.

'Really, sir! You can hardly expect me to perform a clinical examination on a lady with you in the same room.'

'I'm sure Mrs Yarborough wouldn't object in the slightest.'

'Lancelot!' Dulcie drew the bedclothes up to her chin. 'The doctor might ask me to take my nightie off.'

'Oh, very well, very well.' Glaring at Dr Runchleigh, he opened the cabin door. 'I shall take a few turns round the deck. I hope you will be sure of having warm hands before touching her.'

Sir Lancelot shut the cabin door behind him. He looked up and down the ship's alleyway. No one in sight. He quietly applied his ear to the flimsy woodwork.

'I must say, Mrs Yarborough, though he is a knight – or says he is, there is no way of telling aboard, and passengers frequently assume titles to which they are not in the slightest entitled – I find him a man of disconcertingly rough manners.'

'Oh, I expect he spends a lot of time in the company of rather earthy vets. He's a son of the soil, you know. You can hardly expect to find social niceties in a man who spends his entire life rearing pigs.'

'Pigs!' Dr Runchleigh sounded disgusted.

'I'm sure he's got a kind heart underneath. And I quite believe he's taken a fancy to me.'

'To *you*, Mrs Yarborough. It's really quite remarkable the effect the sea has on some of our more elderly passengers. It is, I believe, due to the gentle movement of the ship upon their glands. I hope he is not unduly molesting you? I could always speak to the captain.'

'Don't do that, doctor. I'm enjoying it.'

'I'm afraid these days we don't get the type of passenger I am used to. It is beyond me how some of them afford the fare. The football pools, I expect. Now, my dear Mrs Yarborough, we'll have you right as rain in no time. Just tell me what's the matter, in your own words.'

'I've got a pain in my tummy.'

'Indeed? A dietary indiscretion, perhaps? We partook of the lobster thermidor last night at dinner? Will you please pull up your nightdress, lie down with your arms at your side, breathe regularly and relax. Then I shall be able to perform my examination.'

The cabin door fell away from Sir Lancelot. He staggered on to the carpet. He found himself looking up at Dr Runchleigh, who was holding the handle and glaring.

'Well?' asked Dr Runchleigh bleakly. 'I thought you were taking a turn round the deck?'

Sir Lancelot got slowly to his feet. Dulcie was staring open-mouthed. He exchanged glances with both of them. For once, he was at a loss. 'I thought I'd left my morning paper.'

'The morning paper is not delivered in the middle of the Atlantic, Sir Lancelot.'

'No, you're quite right,' he agreed. He stood stroking his beard.

'It is very fortunate I suspected you were spying on us, Sir Lancelot. I have managed to save Mrs Yarborough from considerable embarrassment.'

He gave a feeble smile. 'It's my dear old fussy nature. I wanted to see everything was all right.'

'You would not seem to have much faith in my morals.'

He looked horrified. 'How could you possibly imagine that?'

'Because you do not seem anxious to leave me alone with a lady patient. If that is the case, I shall have no hesitation in lodging a complaint with the captain.'

'For God's sake, calm down,' Sir Lancelot told him urgently. 'I just thought you might want a hand, that's all.'

'A hand? If I did, I have a hospital orderly down below who is a full member of the St John Ambulance Brigade. Will you please leave us in peace, so that I may continue with my examination?'

'Come back afterwards,' Dulcie invited amiably enough.

The door shut. Sir Lancelot marched away. He leant on the ship's rail, staring gloomily at the ocean. 'They must think I'm dead kinky,' he reflected. 'A sort of surgical peeping Tom.' He stroked his beard for some time. 'Abdominal pain, fever, pulse-rate over ninety . . . H'm. I hope to God that quack isn't too gentlemanly to omit putting a finger up, that's all.'

15

THAT Tuesday was for the dean an unexpected day in the country.

At ten-thirty he drove his Rolls through the elaborate, crested iron gates of Widmore Park, a huge, sleek golf course on the southern outskirts of London, its well-nurtured greens, painstakingly clipped fairways, carefully raked bunkers and splendidly stocked bar at weekends carrying a heavier traffic of stockbrokers than Throgmorton Street in the rush hour.

It was another bright, hot morning, with the sun – as Auberon Dougal might have put it – a ring of toasted cheese in a hungrily empty sky. But the beauty of the green slopes and shapely trees escaped the dean, as he parked and made for the portcullis of the club house. He was irritated, frustrated and worried.

First, he had abandoned his ward-round at St Swithin's to his registrar, and though his patients would not in any way suffer, a conscientious man like himself disliked shirking any duty. Secondly came the case of Mrs Samantha Dougal, who at that moment, he reflected, would be standing penitently in Greek Street Court petitioning a remand on bail. Thirdly and above all, the reception for the Queen was as sadly unrehearsed as the hospital's Christmas Gilbert and Sullivan performances two days before curtain rise.

It would never do if anything in the slightest went even faintly awry with the Queen, the dean reflected, sweat breaking out on the back of his neck again. Or he would never see the inside of the Royal Household in his life. He could imagine a Lord-in-Waiting mentioning to a Gentleman Usher, 'Whatever happened to that doctor fellow Lychfield, who was supposed to be joining us? Haven't seen him about the household anywhere.' 'But didn't you know? He was responsible for the ghastly business in that hospital, when Her Majesty got stuck in the lift and they had to send for Number Twelve Commando to get her out.' 'Really? What a shame we've abolished the rack.' The sweat got worse.

'I'm looking for a Mr Humphrey Fletcher-Boote,' the dean asked a member, in the baronial hall of the golf club. 'He's playing here today in the Bench v Bar match.'

'I should try the locker-room. It's through the picture gallery.'

'Thank you.'

The dean found the eminent criminal lawyer almost hidden by an enormous bag of golf clubs, wearing a brand-new pair of orange slacks, a green shirt and a long-peaked cap. He looked like a professional golfer on television, if twice the weight. 'Ah, there you are,' he greeted the dean. 'Lose yourself?'

'I came as soon as I possibly could.'

'Sorry to drag you all the way down here. But when I was picked for the Bar team, quite obviously that came first. Even the villains at the Old Bailey will have to get on without me today, which is going to cost someone a few years, I'm afraid.' He stared. 'Are you going ratting afterwards?'

'I understood that one wore one's tweeds on a golf course.' The dean sounded offended. 'I've already had one argument about my suit this morning with Josephine.'

'I remember it, don't I? From the days we were undergraduates at Cambridge.' It had been originally a gingery hairy tweed with a purple overcheck, but with time it had suffered extensive alopecia areata, requiring extensive leatherwork and darning by Josephine to cover the bald patches. 'We'd better get moving to the first tee.'

'But I haven't told you anything yet about poor Mrs Samantha Dougal,' protested the dean.

'Brief me as we go round. We can't keep old Crocker waiting.'

'Who's old Crocker?'

'My opponent. A judge. Surely you've heard of him?' The dean shook his head irritably. 'Oh, he's a delightful old character. We're all terribly fond of him. Quite lovable. At heart, that is. He tends to be rather outspoken, admittedly. And perhaps he's a little set in his views. But none of us are perfect, are we? The country needs more judges like him. Would you mind carrying my clubs?'

'What! All those?'

'They're only a standard set. There seems to be a shortage of those trolley things.'

As the dean shouldered the bag, they made towards the sunlit course. 'You really must discuss the case of Mrs Samantha Dougal – '

'Old Crocker can get a shade impatient if he's kept waiting. In court sometimes he throws books and things at the usher.' Mr Fletcher-Boote chuckled. 'Quite Pickwickian. Such a pity his type is dying out. By the way, I shouldn't say much to him, not for the first few holes. He always disagrees with everything anyone says before the luncheon adjournment.'

The QC strode towards the first tee, idly swinging

his driver. The dean staggered after with the clubs. Waiting for them was a short, round, white-haired figure in tweed plus-fours and a white linen jacket. 'You're late, Boote.'

'Sorry, judge. Had to wait for this chap.'

The judge swivelled on the dean an eye as hard and vinegary as a pickled onion. 'You don't look very strong. How old are you? About sixty, I suppose? I expect you drink. Well, let's get going. I'll take the honour.'

Drawing one of four clubs from a narrow canvas golf-bag, Mr Justice Crocker hit his ball squarely down the middle of the fairway with a driver which had twine trailing from the heel. The dean waited with rising impatience as Mr Fletcher-Boote, after a flurry of practice swings, hit his the same distance but at forty-five degrees from the intended direction.

'I *must* start telling you about my sister-in-law,' the dean began urgently, as he and the QC made towards a clump of gorse bushes.

'Your sister-in-law? What about your sister-in-law?'

'My sister-in-law is Mrs Samantha Dougal.'

'Oh, her. Shoplifting, did you say? I'm afraid I wasn't very *compos mentis* when you telephoned so early this morning. Last night was the annual dinner of the Old Lags' Association. Frightful pissup. Why doesn't she just plead guilty, pay her ten quid, and forget about it? She's hardly been shooting her way into the Bank of England.'

The dean shifted the clubs to his other shoulder. 'But surely you understand? A conviction will completely shatter her career for ever. Not to mention undoing much of the good she's performed in the world.'

The QC had his mind on other things. 'Oh, I don't

know. Couldn't she turn it to some use? "My lapse and a real understanding of human problems." That sort of thing. The newspapers would pay handsomely, I expect. Anyway, it won't make any difference if she's acquitted. The British public invariably assume that anyone accused of anything always did it. Ah, there's my ball. Not a bad lie, in the circumstances.' He started picking through the clubs on the dean's back. 'Do you suppose if I took a number six, and quite deliberately hooked it, I could get past those bushes and on to the green?'

'I'm afraid I know nothing whatever about golf,' said the dean tersely.

'Really?' The QC looked amazed. 'Then what did you want to come down and caddy for?'

'I did *not* want to come down here at all. I came specifically to seek your advice about Mrs Samantha Dougal. You really must help her. I explicitly promised her as much.'

'I was forgetting, this was a conference as well as a golf match.' He selected his number six iron. 'Which magistrate's court?'

'Greek Street.'

'Oh, dear.' He flexed his wrists. 'Greek Street is frightfully hot on shoplifting these days, with all the Oxford Street trade. Tough as nails. I'd opt for the Gestapo any day. They'll quite likely send her to jail.'

The ball neatly skirted the bushes, sailed over a bunker and landed exactly on the edge of the green. The QC turned with a broad smile. 'Not bad. In fact, I doubt whether any of your open champions could do much better. What's this you were nattering about? Shoplifting at Greek Street? Oh, don't worry about that. I could go along and get her off in my sleep. Let's catch up old Crocker.'

Somewhat heartened, the dean followed under his load of clubs. The judge too had reached the green. He turned an acid glance on him. 'Flag.'

'I beg your pardon?'

'The flag. Take it out of the hole.' He banged his putter into the turf. 'Haven't you the first idea how to behave on a golf course?'

'I'm extremely sorry,' said the dean hastily, dropping the bag of clubs.

The judge gave a howl. 'You fool. You clumsy oaf. Dropping a heavy bag of clubs right in the middle of the green like that. You'll make it look like a ploughed field before you've finished.'

The dean's mouth tightened. But he obediently reshouldered the clubs. After all, this was Humphrey Fletcher-Boote's friend, however peculiar. He pulled up a flag on the end of a pole. He supposed it was the right one, as there didn't seem another in sight.

From the next tee the QC drove far and straight, explaining to the dean as they walked that magistrates regarded shoplifting in the present age as no crime at all, but the merest lapse of discipline, like speeding. As his next shot dropped into a bunker beside a pond, he was inclined to think this lax attitude towards persons who robbed innocent shopkeepers was undergoing an abrupt and severe change. The judge meanwhile continued to glare at the dean and shout.

'Where did she do it?' Mr Humphrey Fletcher-Boote asked as they approached the second green.

'Plushroses. Caviar and knickers.'

'Dear old Plushroses!' The QC smiled, as if recalling some holiday haunt. 'The number of cases I've handled of gentlefolk misbehaving in Plushroses. Extraordinarily lucrative. Covers my account there. Stopped outside, was she? That woman detective? Front door?' The dean nodded. 'Pity. Back door's a bit strange. Part of the pavement's owned by the shop. You haven't yet left the premises, you see? Got a colonel's lady off with that one.'

'She also beat up a policeman.'

'We'll make a complaint of police brutality. That's the usual drill these days. Any emotional upset?'

'Her husband had just left her.'

'Ah! Splendid.' Mr Fletcher-Boote's putt at the edge of the green reached a couple of feet from the hole. 'Send her to a psychiatrist. Can do?'

'Easily. St Swithin's is full of them.'

'Mind, keep it simple. None of your Oedipus complexes and so on, or you'll confuse the bench, which is invariably fatal.' He tapped the ball into the hole. 'I'll get her off, no trouble at all. With sympathetic words from the bench, too, if we're lucky.'

'Hey. You.' The judge pushed his bag into the dean's arms. 'You can carry that for the next sixteen. I don't see why I should exhaust myself when we've got you with us.'

The dean drew himself up. 'As far as I am concerned, you can stick your beastly clubs up your nares.'

'How *dare* you speak to me in that disrespectful way!'

'Why shouldn't I? You've been speaking to me in a disrespectful way since I set eyes on you.'

'*What* is the world coming to? I remember when the caddies at this club knew their place.'

'This isn't a caddy,' Mr Fletcher-Boote interrupted mildly.

The judge continued to glare. 'Well, if he isn't a caddy, what's he doing wearing a suit like that?'

'With respect, my friend is an eminent physician.' The QC's voice assumed the mellifluence which magically wafted prisoners from the eager fingers of the law, or – if he were being paid on the occasion by the Crown – pitched them neck and crop into the cells. 'It was his only opportunity to discuss with me the sad case of a distant relative charged with shop-lifting, my friend being as overwhelmed with his arduous professional responsibilities almost as completely as you yourself, m'lud, I mean Charles.'

The judge looked faintly more cheerful. 'Shoplifting? I take it your client – I mean, your caddy – has read my article in *Punishment*?'

'I would ask leave to doubt that.'

'I'm obliged. The essence of shoplifting, of any form of larceny, whether of a bar of chocolate or a bar of gold, is the intention, expressed by the action, that the taker intends permanently to deprive the owner of his rightful goods. *Ipso facto* – Caddy, my driver. Caddy! Where's that bloody caddy of yours got to?'

But the dean had thrown the clubs in a bunker and was hurrying for home.

16

WEDNESDAY morning. Barely twenty-four hours to go. The dean wished that he were several thousand miles away, inaccessibly surrounded by ocean. Even in the company of Sir Lancelot.

His first worry was the weather. After weeks of blazing sunshine, the BBC had with its usual irritating nannyishness warned that morning of punishment to come, with thunder, lightning and hailstorms. It would never do if they got the Queen wet. His second concern was the apparent impossibility of organizing a rehearsal in St Swithin's at all. His third was still Samantha, who was waiting for him in the marbled hall, as at nine sharp he approached the automatic doors rubbing his hands with none of his usual briskness.

'Lionel – '

'Samantha – '

They touched finger-tips. The dean felt that someone had connected him up to the hospital mains. She looked lovely in distress. Her auburn hair glistened as excitingly as ever, but there was a new softness about her, the dean thought, as though she had been scraped of a layer of enamel.

'I'm sorry my telephone message asked you to be here so early,' the dean continued. 'How did it go yesterday in Greek Street?'

'Your solicitor was most helpful. It was all over in a minute. Remanded on bail till Tuesday fortnight. As no doubt you have seen splashed all over this morning's newspapers.' She shuddered. 'They were awful in Greek Street. The bay of a jackal sniffing blood is nothing to the whoop of a reporter spotting feet of clay.'

'But I have a ray of hope, Samantha. More than a ray. Indeed, the sun is rising on the black night of your despair. In the body of Mr Humphrey Fletcher-Boote, QC. As a special favour he's agreed to take your case, and actually appear at Greek Street himself. I'd have told you sooner, but had to make absolutely sure last night on the telephone. He had various other preoccupations earlier in the day.'

Her face glowed with relief. 'Do you think he can get an acquittal?'

'Acquittal? Of course. He gave the impression of a Wimbledon champion going down for a knock-up at the local tennis club.'

'Lionel, how can I ever thank you?' she asked breathlessly.

'Please. It only embarrasses me. By the way, you have to see a psychiatrist.'

'Oh.' Her face fell again.

'I'm sorry, but Fletcher-Boote insists.'

'But I've never even thought of consulting one before.'

'It's nothing to be ashamed of. And you'll find Dr M'Turk most helpful and sympathetic. I'm sure.'

'Who's Dr M'Turk?'

'The psychiatrist. A lady. She looks a bit pre-Raphaelite, but she's extremely sound at her job. Auberon is most impressed with her.'

'Auberon? What's Auberon had to do with her?'

'Oh . . . well, you see Dr M'Turk and her husband live in the house next door to me. So Auberon's noticed her going in and out. He was impressed. She's a very impressive woman. Particularly from a distance.'

Samantha's lower lip trembled. 'And how is Auberon?'

'Fine. A little moody, of course. Only to be expected. He's going out to lunch today with his publisher's editor at the Garrick Club. I must say, he seems to do nothing but eat extravagant meals with various literary figures. It must be a terribly unhealthy life, being an author. I suppose quite a lot of them drop dead from obesity and alcoholism.'

Samantha fell silent. The dean scratched his ear. He thought it a brilliant idea of his, sending Samantha to the same psychiatrist as her husband. After even a superficial study of Auberon's psychology, the dean felt, Dr M'Turk could express with quite overpowering conviction her opinion that Samantha's mental health had been undermined by her spouse. Such an unusual opportunity to place every possible fact in the psychiatrist's hands must be seized. No detail could be overlooked, not after his trouble in getting Humphrey Fletcher-Boote to appear in Greek Street, quite apart from carrying his blasted golf clubs. And Dr M'Turk herself had jumped with surprising eagerness to his suggestion. Nor was there any chance of either Auberon or Samantha coming to know they shared the same couch. Dr M'Turk had given her assurance of professional secrecy, while the patients themselves weren't even on speaking terms.

The dean looked at his watch. 'I fixed an appointment for you at nine fifteen. I'll take you up. It's quite convenient. Dr M'Turk's clinic is on the top floor, next to my own office.'

They approached the lift. The doors slid apart to emit Professor Oliphant, in his white coat. 'Ah, dean, I congratulate you. The lifts of this building haven't stuck for twenty-four hours. By the way, why can't your super-modern hospital kitchens provide chips? My patients are almost rioting. Surely you know that if Napoleon's army marched on its stomach, the entire British nation slithers on its chips? As for the frozen peas, I have removed tastier-looking objects from many of my patients' gall-bladders.'

He noticed Samantha. 'Good morning, Mrs Dougal. If it is any consolation to you that a prickly and somewhat cynical professor of surgery regards the comments of today's press as loutishly brutal to the point of inhumanity, I hope you will take it. I assure you that my heartfelt sympathy is matched only by my cleverly concealed admiration on many occasions for your moral courage. By the way, dean, another visitor arrived at my house this morning. I am assuming he is a doctor, but as he speaks only Japanese it is somewhat difficult to find out.'

He strode off. The dean blinked. 'You know,' he admitted, 'I don't think that fellow is quite so black as he paints himself.'

They went up. With a reassuring pat, the dean put Samantha through Dr M'Turk's door. He hurried along the corridor, his brain busy with the many remaining problems of the day. There was his house-physician, for a start. Over the last few days the young man had been exhibiting the signs of galloping mental decay. He was probably on drugs. Well, the fellow musn't be allowed to make a scandalous exhibition of himself at the following morning's ceremonies. The dean made a mental note to have him tidied out of the way.

'Good morning, Sir Lionel,' his blonde secretary greeted him from her typewriter. 'The chaplain is waiting inside to see you.'

The dean pulled up short. 'Really, Miss Duffin. Don't you remember my instructions? I absolutely refuse to set eyes on that holy hippie again.'

'Not *him*, Sir Lionel. The proper chaplain. Mr Nosworthy.'

The dean found the Reverend Nosworthy wearing the same green Donegal jacket and MCC tie. He was sitting disconsolately beside the desk, holding his panama hat.

'Well, well, quite a surprise.' The dean gave a brittle smile. 'Up for the day, eh? Makes a change from Whitstable. Delighted to see you any time you happen to be in London. Do just drop in. Though of course you realize that I have an enormous amount of work to get through, and so am very likely to be elsewhere when you call. My secretary will tell you. Perhaps you've brought me some oysters? Or there has to be an "R" in the month for oysters to appear, I believe? Otherwise they are busy breeding. Well, padre, I'm afraid that I am incredibly pressed for time – '

'Sir Lionel.' He opened his arms imploringly. 'I'm in a terrible state. You must save me.'

The dean eyed him sternly. 'You haven't been shoplifting, too?'

'Shoplifting? Oh, dear me, no. I could never do anything like that. It is simply that Whitstable is getting me down.'

'But damn it! You've only been there six days.'

'Alas, it seems more like six years.'

'And Whitstable is, as I understand it, a most agreeable town, with sea breezes and an interesting view of the shipping in the Thames estuary. I should jump at the chance of retiring there myself.'

'I suppose Whitstable is all right,' the Reverend

Nosworthy admitted glumly. 'Though to a man of even my most limited means and amusements, a trifle dull after London. And I suppose my boarding-house is passable, even if it looks on to the railway line and is somewhat ungenerous in the matter of sugar and hot water. But unfortunately – and I should perhaps have suspected it before making my choice – the house is full of other retired clergymen.'

'Well, move somewhere else,' the dean told him impatiently, starting to arrange the papers on his desk. 'Now, if you will excuse me – '

'But my dear dean!' The clergyman's jowls shook. 'The whole of Whitstable is full of retired clergymen. Perhaps the proximity to Canterbury has something to do with it. I just don't know where to turn. Or rather, I do.' He paused. 'I want to come back here. *This* is my home.'

'Impossible. As much as I should like to get rid of your successor – who to my mind is unsuited to be chaplain even to a teenagers' pop festival – I can't see how I can. If the bishop appoints Mr Becket here, that seems to me the end of it. I can't presume to tell the bishop what to do. Even though I have no high opinion of bishops who let their hair grow and play the guitar in public.'

The Reverend Nosworthy stared hard at his brown boots. 'The appointment is nothing to do with My Lord the bishop.'

'You prefer to pin the responsibility on the League of Friends and Mrs Samantha Dougal?' The dean opened a file, and clicked his ballpoint several times. 'Of course, the bishop takes her advice. They must be pretty thick, when she lets him appear on her television programme. I'm afraid you really must let me get on with my day's work.'

'Nor is it anything to do with those muddle-headed ladies in the League of Friends. The appointment of the hospital chaplain rest with one man.' The Reverend Nosworthy looked at the dean closely. 'A man who is decisive, learned, well respected, and though much criticized constantly at the service of his fellows.'

'The Prime Minister?'

'You.' The dean frowned. 'You are perhaps familiar with advowsons, Sir Lionel? The rights of patronage, a relic from the days of squire and parson. Perhaps no bad thing, I often think. Some ten thousand ecclesiastical livings are still, I believe, in the hands of private individuals. Some large property speculators today could if they wished deploy an army of clergymen. This hospital is also the ancient parish of St Swithin's Without – as you know. And the power to appoint its incumbent has since the last century been vested in the dean of the medical school – as perhaps you don't. I'm afraid I kept rather quiet about it,' the Reverend Nosworthy admitted. 'You see, for years I was afraid that you might kick me out.'

The dean tapped his teeth thoughtfully with the butt of his ballpoint. 'So I could simply tell the bishop that he had no right to appoint Becket, and invite you back?'

Mr Nosworthy nodded. 'Indeed you could.'

'It might upset Mrs Samantha Dougal . . . on the other hand, by next Sunday the Reverend Becket might quite well be organizing a mass patients' lie-in because they aren't allowed to stay awake for their own operations, or some such.' He tapped his teeth again, rather louder. 'I must admit, I feel diffident in meddling with ecclesiastical matters. It would be exactly the same as my trying to meddle with one of Professor Oliphant's nephrectomies. We cannot be an expert in everything,' the dean conceded. 'I only wish there was someone I could turn to for independent advice.'

The dispossessed chaplain fixed him with a watery eye. 'One other member of the consultant staff knew about the advowson. I'm afraid he somehow got to know everybody's secrets. Though we had our little disagreements over the years – he imagined for some reason that I had no right to go to the lavatory – I felt he was sorry to see me go. He disliked all modernization and I am sure he would particularly dislike it embodied in Becket.'

'Sir Lancelot Spratt? But he's floating about, miles away.'

'Could you not cable?' The Reverend Nosworthy crumpled his panama pathetically. 'I would even be prepared to pay. At night rates, of course.'

17

'PLEASE sit down,' Dr M'Turk indicated the red-covered couch with a brief gesture.

'I believe Sir Lionel has told you something about my case,' began Samantha nervously.

'A little. But I am not quite clear exactly what crime you committed. I gathered that it was robbery with violence.'

'Oh, no. It was shoplifting. And assaulting the police. Only one policeman, of course.'

'Perhaps Sir Lionel has a tendency for exaggeration.' Dr M'Turk opened a blue cardboard file. 'Well, we had better start at the beginning. Age?'

'Thirty.'

'Really? I should have thought you much older than that. You must tell me the exact truth, you know, however painful. Only frankness will get us anywhere.'

Samantha looked at the floor. She said quietly, 'I believe that beauty is truth, truth beauty.'

'I see you read Bartlett's *Familiar Quotations*. Married, widowed or divorced?'

'Married. My husband is Auberon Dougal. The writer.'

'What *sort* of writer?'

Samantha looked up. 'He's the novelist.' She added with a flicker of pride, 'Perhaps you've read some of his work?'

'I can't say that I've heard of his books. But I'll ask our *au pair* girl. She reads all sorts of stuff. And you?'

'Me?'

'Yes. What do you do? If anything.'

'But I'm Mrs Samantha Dougal,' she explained, unbelievingly.

'I already have your name. I am inquiring your occupation.'

Samantha laid her hands submissively in her lap. 'You may perhaps have seen me on television.'

'We *have* a set at home. It's worthwhile for Wimbledon and the archaeology programmes. But of course, I never watch any of the entertainment. The whole of life today is, I find, a struggle to avoid being entertained. You're BBC Two? Not BBC One? Commercial! Oh dear.'

'I'm afraid you don't quite understand,' Samantha continued in a crushed voice. 'I am not a performer. I take the chair in various discussions on uplifting subjects. At the moment I am trying desperately to improve the sexual outlook of the nation.'

'Aren't we all, dearie?'

Samantha bit her lip. This strange woman doctor was really most abrasive. She felt that Lionel might at least have warned her. But she had to abase herself. It was the result which counted. To obtain a medical report which, in Mr Fletcher-Boote's wizardly hands at Greek Street, would ensure her acquittal Samantha was prepared to face any humiliation. And for all she knew, psychiatrists throughout the country treated their patients in the same way. 'Please ask me exactly what you wish.'

'Don't worry, I shall. Now to the family history. How many of your relatives are insane?'

Samantha considered. 'Only one. An auntie. She imagined she was a telephone box.'

'How extraordinary. Was she treated?'

'I don't think so. It was in the country, where people don't seem to bother overmuch about such things. My aunt just used to stand about on street corners. She could never understand why nobody ever made a call from her.'

'Your education. What sort of school?'

'Boarding school. On the Norfolk coast.'

'Involved in Lesbian practices from an early age, I suppose?'

Samantha coloured. 'I certainly was not.'

'Really? Hard luck. I should have imagined you'd have been quite attractive. Let us move on to adult life. We'll draw up a complete list of your extramarital sexual activities. Heterosexual ones first.'

Samantha eyed her steadily. 'There have been absolutely none. Of either variety.'

Dr M'Turk made a note. 'Patient lacks initiative. Very well. How about the premarital ones?'

'None.'

'Think.'

'I said none.'

'Think again.'

Samantha momentarily shut her eyes. 'Well – '

'Yes?'

'There was a theological student one Whitsun in Scunthorpe.'

'Was he nice?'

Samantha averted her head. 'He had a moustache and metal-rimmed glasses and a bicycle.'

Dr M'Turk made another note. 'How Freud would have enjoyed that! Smoking, drinking and drugs?'

'None.'

'Lucky you. About your husband. Sir Lionel says he's just left you.'

'That is correct. Though I know that he still loves me.'

Dr M'Turk glared. 'On what grounds are you making that assumption? We shall have to go into it, won't we? What was your sex life like with him?'

'How do you mean?' asked Samantha falteringly.

'Well, was your husband a satisfactory partner?'

'*Most* satisfactory indeed.'

Dr M'Turk raised her eyebrows. 'He was a man of stamina?'

'By that you mean . . . oh, yes. Oh, yes, indeed. Of great stamina.'

'Splendid. I mean, how splendid for you.'

'Sometimes all the way through the last movement of Beethoven's Fifth Symphony.'

Dr M'Turk stared. 'You did it to music?'

'My husband said it was like wine with food. I think he was something of an accomplished hedonist.'

'Any other perversions? Chains and padlocks? Firemen's helmets? Jumping off the wardrobe? No? Well, Mrs Dougal. I understood from Sir Lionel Lychfield – what's your relationship with *him*, by the way?'

'We are good friends.'

'H'm,' said Dr M'Turk doubtfully. 'Be that as it may, you want me to write a letter saying that, in my professional opinion, your mental health is of such delicacy that your lapse into shoplifting can be explained and excused by the trauma of your husband's absconding. That's roughly it?'

'I should much appreciate that, doctor.'

Dr M'Turk tapped her finger tips together. 'Mrs Dougal, if all shoplifters were acquitted simply by some gullible doctor certifying that they were psychopaths, the counters of the West End of London would in no time at all be as bare as the surface of the moon. No,

Mrs Dougal. I am afraid that I have come to the conclusion that you are mentally perfectly normal. The only thing wrong is your being a self-satisfied prig. Good morning.'

Samantha stood up. 'Good morning, Dr M'Turk,' she said with dignity. 'I must thank you for the attention you have given me. I am sorry if I have occupied too much of your time. Time which you could have given to others whom you would consider more deserving than myself.'

She left the room. She pressed the button for the lift. She did not want to see Lionel. Or anyone. Except Auberon.

Staring fixedly ahead, Samantha went down to the hall. Unseeingly she crossed the terrazzo floor and made her way through the automatic doors and among the cars in the forecourt. She turned the corner into Lazar Row. After that humiliating half hour, all she wanted was comfort, reassurance and an emergency transfusion of flattery for her battered self-esteem.

She rang the dean's doorbell. Faith answered it.

'Hello, Auntie Samantha. Uncle Auberon's just gone out. He's got a lunch date, but he had to have a drink with a film actress in the Causerie Bar at Claridge's Hotel first. He's always busy dashing out for his lunches and dinners. It must be lovely, being an author.'

Samantha looked disappointed. 'Is your mother at home?'

'No one but me, I'm afraid, auntie. I say, you don't look very well. Wouldn't you like to come in and have a cup of coffee and some chocolate biscuits?'

'I think coffee is exactly what I need.'

Faith shut the front door behind them. 'I saw you on the telly last Sunday, auntie,' she continued eagerly. 'You were smashing.'

'Thank you, thank you, dear Faith.' Samantha felt

that no praise had been more welcome in her lifetime. 'That's very heartening.'

'Even Miss Clitworth used to like your programmes, though she said television insulted her intelligence. She used to watch a lot, really, with her study door locked. When the violence came on she used to get quite excited. I looked through her net curtains.'

They went into the kitchen. As Faith put a kettle on the stove, Samantha sat wearily at the pink-topped table. 'I suppose you heard I've been rather naughty?'

Faith opened an elaborately coloured tin of chocolate biscuits. '*I* don't think so. If shops don't want you to pinch things, why do they always lay everything out so invitingly?'

Samantha bit into a biscuit. 'I'm afraid that's no excuse.'

'Anyway, daddy says you did it only because you were mentally upset at the time.' Faith spooned coffee powder into two mugs. 'Over uncle.'

'Unfortunately, that isn't an excuse, either. I wasn't mentally upset at the time. Or rather, *I'm* quite sure I was. But my own opinion in the matter is of course perfectly valueless. I've just been told that I am absolutely normal in all respects by a qualified psychiatrist.'

'Dr M'Turk.' Faith poured in the boiling water. 'She lives next door. She's awfully weird. We had a mistress like her at school. She used to keep gerbils in her bedroom, but one day they all ate each other.'

They sat at the table, both sipping their coffee. 'Of course you're sane, auntie. As sane as Miss Clitworth at school.'

'I suppose I should be grateful for it. Particularly in these dreadful days, when there is so much mental instability about.'

'In the school play last Christmas, Miss Clitworth

played Ophelia. She was jolly good, too. Still, it was a pity that Hamlet and all the men had to be girls. Even the ghost.'

'Performances of the wholesome classics are a most valuable part of English education.'

'Miss Clitworth went mad. In her big scene. She had us all frightened, the way she was rolling her eyes and dribbling. But of course, she was only pretending.'

'So I should hope, Faith.'

'And why shouldn't you?'

Samantha stared hard. 'But that's quite ridiculous, child.'

'No, it isn't, auntie. I'm sure psychiatrists like Dr M'Turk make lots of mistakes. Daddy says they're even worse than the weather forecasters. But if you pretended you were mad good and proper, everyone would agree and be awfully sorry for you.'

Samantha laughed. 'What would you suggest I do? I can hardly follow Ophelia by throwing myself into the Thames at Battersea Bridge and floating downstream with a garland of flowers from Constance Spry.'

'It's simple, auntie. You take all your clothes off.'

Samantha started. 'Outrageous.'

'Not if you're mad. A lot of people do, when they go crazy. It's one of the very first signs, I expect. Daddy could probably tell you. There was a girl in our dorm at school who walked down the High Street starkers. Miss Clitworth had to send out the school Guide patrol with blankets. Poor thing, they had to take her away. But I think she only did it to get out of her O levels.'

Samantha gave an indulgent smile. 'All right, my dear Faith. You *are* one for bright ideas, aren't you? But suppose I *did* wish to impress the world that I was raving mad by wandering about naked? Where and when, in this unbelievably permissive age, could I possibly achieve that object?'

'Easy. In the main hall of St Swithin's tomorrow, at twelve-thirty.'

'And why, may I ask, that particular place and time?'

'Because that's when the Queen's coming to receive a golden key from daddy to open the new building.'

'Of course! I was forgetting, with all my troubles.' There was a long silence. Samantha drank her coffee. 'Out of the question. Quite out of the question. I have far too high esteem for your father.'

Faith looked hurt. 'I was only trying to help, auntie.'

'I know you were, my child, I appreciate your simple, girlish view of the problem. It is pleasant that you can still be blinded by the light of your own innocence.' She drank more coffee. 'What time, as a matter of interest, did you say Her Majesty was arriving?'

'Twelve-thirty, auntie. Tomorrow.'

'Do you know, I think I'll have another of those scrumptious chocolate biscuits. Where does your mother get them from?'

'Plushroses, auntie.'

'H'm,' said Samantha.

18

'CABLE, sir.'

Sir Lancelot turned. For a long moment he eyed the envelope on the silver salver. 'Better open it, I suppose.' he decided. 'It might always be from my bookmaker.'

He adjusted his half-moon glasses.

DO YOU REPEAT YOU KNOW AMUSING STORY NOT REPEAT NOT RE SIGMOIDOSCOPES AND GLASS EYES QUERY FURTHERMORE CHAPLAIN DOESNT LIKE WHITSTABLE CAN I GIVE HIM ST SWITHINS QUERY NOT TO MENTION MRS SAMANTHA DOUGAL HAS BEEN RUINED IN PLUSHROSES TO CAP ALL WHERE IS BLOODY GOLDEN KEY QUERY OLIPHANT SAYS IN BANK ISNT WHY DO YOU NOT SPEAK TO ME QUERY AM SPENDING A FORTUNE SENDING YOU CABLES YOU HAVE NO IDEA HOW EXPENSIVE IT IS PER WORD HOPE HAVING CALM SEA LIONEL

Sir Lancelot turned the flimsy over. Taking a pencil from the inner pocket of his white dinner jacket, he wrote on the back,

LYCHFIELD TWO LAZAR ROW LONDON NO YES REALLY DONT KNOW SORRY YES LANCELOT

'Have that dispatched, steward.' He handed the man a tip. 'And, steward – '

'Sir?'

'Please tell the wireless office that if any more communications emanate from the very obviously deranged mind of my poor friend in London, I should be obliged if they would kindly save them up and hand them over when I step down the gangway at the end of the voyage.'

Sir Lancelot turned back, elbows on the teak rail, gazing over the flat moonlit sea. He was alone, sipping a whisky and soda. From the floodlit upper deck floated the strains of a waltz by Lehar, punctuated by the distant brisk strokes of the ship's bell. It was that time in mid-evening when the passengers were presumed to have digested their eight-course dinner and be ravenous for the lobster and turkey sandwiches served by the stewards at eleven.

Sir Lancelot felt he was enjoying himself hugely. The unexacting, inflexible routine of life on a cruise – which he supposed had hardly changed since the leisurely nineteen-thirties when they were invented – was surprisingly soothing after the rush of St Swithin's. There was admittedly a pop group aboard, but they were a gesture by the shipping line and made miserable opposition to the bingo, old tyme dancing and going to sleep in deckchairs. A lot of the passengers were his own age and many a good deal older – the vessel was a well appointed geriatric playground, he thought, with the extra attraction of drinks at duty-free prices.

'Lancelot, there you are. I've been looking all round the smoking room.'

Dulcie Yarborough joined him, a sable wrap over her shoulders.

'I was seeking a little solitude for thought. And seclusion is the only item in short supply on this ship.'

She leant on the rail beside him, with a little shiver. 'It's turning chilly, don't you think?'

'Is it? I thought it was somewhat stifling tonight.' He shot her a keen glance under his bristly eyebrows. 'I hope you are feeling better after your day in bed yesterday?'

'Yes, I think Dr Runchleigh did me a power of good.' She paused, giving a wince. 'Yes, I'm feeling fine, absolutely splendid.'

Sir Lancelot sipped his whisky. He recognized that he had worked himself into an insolubly tricky situation. The greatest relaxation of all aboard was his being – for the first time in his mature life – an ordinary human. Persons could not trap him in a corner to solicit advice on their rheumatic hip or their wife's indifference, or their tendency to lose control of their appetites, their children or their bladders. A medical man is a wishing well into which everyone drops his symptoms in the hope of instant relief. But being a pig farmer had disadvantages. It left him powerless to relieve his deep professional concern over the health of the lady leaning on the rail beside him.

Of course, he could apply the pig farmer with the humane killer, he thought, stroking his beard as they listened in silence to the distant music. He could tell Dulcie straight out that he was a surgeon, and take over her treatment. But unfortunately she was already Dr Runchleigh's patient. For himself to intrude would be a flagrant breach of professional ethics. And from his limited experience of the ship's doctor, the horrible fellow would report him to the General Medical Council the day they reached port, if not cable them at once.

'I don't believe anyone should give in easily to illness, Lancelot.'

He didn't hear. And after all, Sir Lancelot told himself, I may well be wrong about Dulcie and the ship's doctor right. Let's face it, he's examined her and I haven't. I'm not in the position even to express an opinion. As I've drummed into my students for years, making a diagnosis before thoroughly examining the case is a trap fatal to both the patient and the doctor's reputation.

'Lancelot, you're dreaming.'

'I do apologize. It's the romantic night.'

'I just said I didn't believe anyone should give in easily to illness. My second husband taught me that. He once danced all night through at a hunt ball with a broken leg. Would you like to try a step or two? Though I do wish ship's orchestras would occasionally learn something other than Viennese waltzes.'

Sir Lancelot said nothing for a moment. Then he drew his face close to hers. 'Dulcie, I love you.'

She looked startled. Then she smiled. 'It's just the moonlight and the water, isn't it?'

'Not a bit. Of course, a ship in a hot climate behaves like a pressure cooker for romance. They're famous for it. But I loved you as soon as I set eyes on you. In the harbour at Tenerife, which was in broad daylight and extremely smelly.'

'Well . . . that's certainly very flattering.'

'It's no mere flattery, Dulcie, I assure you. I throb with passion. Right through.'

She drew the sables closer round her shoulders. 'I must admit, Lancelot, I've been waiting for you to say something like that.'

'Oh?'

'You see, I have grown very, very fond of you. I can't deny it. Anyway, I wouldn't want to.'

'That is deeply gratifying.'

'I always have had an affection for the out-door type of man.'

'Have you?' He sounded disappointed. 'Oh, the pig farm. Yes. You must come and see it. I'm sure you'll love it.'

'But you said you'd sold it.'

'Did I? Perhaps I said I'd sold one of them. I have pig farms all over the shop. Right round the country.' He waved a hand expansively. 'I breed all sorts from Wessex Saddleback to Aberdeen Angus.'

'But an Aberdeen Angus is a bull!'

'Let's not talk any more shop.' He drew closer. 'Dulcie, my love . . . my darling . . . how would you react if I suggested that tonight you invited me to your cabin?'

She smiled slowly. 'How strange you should say that.'

'Why?'

'Because I was meaning to, anyway.'

He grabbed her elbow. 'Let's go.'

'Lancelot! Right now?'

'You bet.'

He left his glass of whisky on the deck. He hustled her through the first open doorway. Still gripping her elbow, he hurried along the deck and down the nearest companionway.

'My, you are keen,' she murmured.

'As mustard.'

'Are you like this with all your girlfriends?'

'No. Only on this particular occasion.' He glanced round. 'Which is our quickest route?'

'But I'm out of breath already.'

'No point in wasting time.'

'I don't know *what* sort of a state I'll be in when you've finished with me,' she said delightedly.

'Here we are.' Sir Lancelot threw open her cabin door. He bundled Dulcie inside, switched on the lights and turned the lock. 'Right. Just lie down on the bunk and take your things off.'

'Lancelot!' She fell back on the cover, eyes half

closed. 'This is terrific. You're so commanding. So masterful. So utterly relentless. Just like my third husband. God, I can't wait.'

She flung her sables on the deck. With almost a single action she ripped off her dress, bra, tights and pants. She lay back on the pillow wearing only her diamond earrings. She had her eyes shut, her chest heaving, her lips pouting, her arms inviting. After half a minute had gone past, she opened her lids again. 'But Lancelot! Aren't you even going to take your trousers off?'

He gave a little smile. 'Mustn't rush things, must we? Much more enjoyable to take our time.'

She leant on her elbow, looking puzzled. 'But a moment ago you were like one of your own rutting boars.'

He advanced to the bunk, his smile more sickly. 'Dulcie, my dear. I have something to confess to you.'

'Yes?' She looked alarmed.

'I have a little peculiarity – '

'Oh, no! Not you too? Are all men kinky these days?'

'Pray do not be over concerned. But I have a fondness – a quite *wholesome* fondness, I like to think – for tickling ladies' tum-tums.'

She still eyed him doubtfully. 'Well, if *that's* all . . . I mean it doesn't sound particularly abnormal. Not compared with some of the things that go on. I don't see why you shouldn't indulge in your little fun.' She hesitated, then lay down again, smiling. 'As a matter of fact, darling, I rather enjoy having my tummy tickled myself. My second husband was very good at it. He had a bristly moustache.'

'Good. Just lie still on your back, breathe quietly and relax.'

Sir Lancelot placed his fingers on the lower right side of her softly-rounded abdomen.

'Ooooooooooch!' She sat up with a jerk. 'That *hurt.*'

'Ah. So it did?'

'You *are* kinky.' She regarded him angrily. 'You're a bloody sadist.'

'If you would kindly let me repeat the manoeuvre – '

'Not likely, I shan't.' She snatched up her dress. 'Get out. Get out of my cabin at once. I don't know what you'll be up to next. I should have had more sense, than risking being alone with a monster like you. The ship's doctor warned me that you were perverted. You kept trying to watch while he examined me.'

'Madam – ' Sir Lancelot's beard bristled. 'I am a surgeon.'

'A likely story! Women get assaulted with that line every week. You've only got to read the Sunday papers. Now get out, before I ring for the stewardess.'

'Madam,' Sir Lancelot continued steadfastly. 'I have just, with considerable ingenuity and trouble, succeeded in palpating your McBurney's point. It confirms precisely the suspicion I formed yesterday morning, when I was trying to supervise Dr Runchleigh's unbelievably inept examination. You are developing acute appendicitis. You will need the best of surgical care, which fortunately I can give.'

She looked confused. 'But if you're a surgeon, why did you say you were a pig farmer?'

'Because, madam, I am sick and tired of continually being at the beck and call of ruddy difficult patients like you. Now listen to me.' His finger pointed below her umbilicus. 'You had a tubal pregnancy some years ago, which blew up and was removed by Sir Gareth de Quincy, the fashionable gynaecologist.'

She gasped. 'How did you know that? I was hardly

sixteen at the time. It was kept a tremendous secret.'

'Because that scar, however faint, could be nothing else. And de Quincy always made an incision like that for his ectopics. Believe me, I've been into a good many abdomens in his footsteps. Well? Now do you believe me?'

'But the ship's doctor said I was only suffering from constipation,' she persisted.

'The ship's doctor is the only man I know who manages to combine so superbly unctuousness and pomposity with howling conceit and abysmal ignorance.'

'He's been giving me cascara for it.'

Sir Lancelot jumped. 'What? Purgatives with a possible appendix? My God! That's fundamental surgical error number one. If a candidate swung that on me in an exam, I'd not only fail him but have him charged with manslaughter.'

She was thoroughly alarmed. 'But what's going to happen to me?'

'Peritonitis,' he told her briefly. 'Listen carefully. You weren't in for dinner?'

'I couldn't face anything.'

'Right. Nothing by mouth henceforward, if you please. I shall be operating in two hours' time. Dr Runchleigh will be administering the anaesthetic, a procedure which I hope is not also beyond his abilities, and which I shall anyway observe with my usual closeness. And don't worry, Dulcie, my dear. I am a consultant surgeon at St Swithin's Hospital – '

'But that's where my last husband went for his vasectomy after he'd left me!'

Sir Lancelot snapped his fingers. 'Of course. Yarborough. Big burly fellow? I performed the operation. He has a . . . a sort of red mole thing, half way down

10

his – ' Dulcie nodded eagerly. '*Now* will you believe me? I'm off to find the ship's doctor.'

'But Lancelot – '

'Yes?' He turned from the door.

'If I hadn't been ill, would you still have wanted to come to my cabin tonight, anyway?'

He bowed courteously. 'In theory, yes. But as a student I never cared to pass the theory and risk failing the practical.'

Sir Lancelot found Dr Runchleigh in bright orange silk pyjamas, going to bed.

'Sorry to disturb your rest, Runchleigh,' Sir Lancelot began, pushing open the cabin door. 'Tell me, are you capable of giving a simple anaesthetic? Ether would probably do, if you're not used to messing about with muscle relaxants. I might even be able to get by with local.'

The ship's doctor stared. 'What a peculiar request! At this time of night, too.'

'In a couple of hours' time I intend to cut into Mrs Yarborough.'

He cowered back across the cabin. 'I knew it. I knew you had this horrible perversion. I warned her. She can't blame me. Don't hurt me. Please don't hurt me. If you want to play Jack the Ripper – '

'I omitted to mention that I am a Master of Surgery and a Fellow of the Royal College. And that I am on at St Swithin's. Please forgive the oversight. Now take me to the ship's operating theatre. I shall want a thorough check of the equipment.'

Dr Runchleigh's mouth fell open. 'But why should I believe all this? You told me you were some sort of pig farmer.'

'I must confess to becoming a little bored this evening

at repeatedly having to establish my credentials. Though doubtless it is all my own fault. This is an emergency, Runchleigh. . . .' Sir Lancelot gave a moment's thought. 'I shall identify myself. Tell me, what are the posterior anatomical relations of the left kidney?'

'I . . . er, don't know. Not offhand, that is.'

'The diaphragm, the quadratus lumborum, the origin of the transversus, the lateral border of the psoas, the subcostal, iliohypogastric and ilioinguinal nerves, and the tips of the transverse processes of the upper three lumbar vertebrae,' Sir Lancelot reeled off. 'What special investigations would you perform in a case of cholelithiasis?'

'I don't fancy I've encountered many instances of the condition.'

'Plain X-ray, oral cholecystogram, intravenous cholangiography, barium meal, liver function tests. How do you treat oesophageal diverticulae?'

Dr Runchleigh held a hand over his eyes. 'Please, Sir Lancelot . . . let's go down to the theatre. I have an absolute horror of viva voce examinations. I failed my surgery finals twenty-two times.'

19

JOSEPHINE woke. Her husband was about to throw himself from their bedroom window.

'Lionel – !' She shot bolt upright. 'Don't. Don't do it. It can't be as bad as that.'

He looked at her blankly. 'What can't?'

'I'm sure it'll go off without a single hitch. I know it was an awful mix up yesterday evening, but everyone says that a terrible dress rehearsal means a wonderful show, don't they? And just think – if you . . . do what you're going to do, you'll spoil the entire day for everyone else at St Swithin's.'

'Do what?'

'Don't jump, Lionel. Think of me, of the children. Think of your patients. Think of the Queen.'

'I happen to be looking at the weather,' the dean told her irritably. He craned out of the window again. 'Last night that peculiar man on the television who seems to have chronic gumboils distinctly forecast storms for later this morning. He's wrong, as usual. The sky is clear blue. All of it. I've just inspected it.'

Josephine glanced anxiously at the electric clock beside her. 'Do come back to bed, dear. You'll need plenty of sleep, to face such a trying day.'

'Sleep? Are you mad, woman? I've a million things awaiting my most urgent attention.'

'But it's only half past five!'

'I must get dressed, get on.' The dean started stripping off his blue and yellow spotted pyjamas. 'Thank God we found that golden key. I do wish you'd reminded me a little earlier that I'd hidden it in the biscuit barrel in my sherry cupboard.'

'Well, *I'm* going back to sleep.'

'Please yourself,' the dean told her airily. 'Just try and be at your place in the main hall at twelve twenty five, if you can.'

The dean showered and shaved, repeating his speech so rapidly, with moving lips and an intense expression, he resembled a conscientious monk at prayer. He went back to the bedroom. He took from his wardrobe the tail-coat, striped trousers and dove grey double-breasted waistcoat for which he was temporarily indebted – like all the St Swithin's consultant staff and most of social-going London that morning – to Mr Moss and his brothers. He dressed with the mixed feelings of a young footballer donning his first English jersey at Wembley and a slightly nervous astronaut preparing for count-down.

Josephine woke from a doze. The dean was fully dressed, pearl pin in grey cravat, grey top hat jauntily on his head, eyeing himself smugly in the mirror. She shot bolt upright again. 'What's the time? I've overslept. Where's the Queen?'

'It really is an effective outfit for formal occasions. Whatever people say, the summer scene would be drabber without it. The time? It's five past six.'

'But you can't go round dressed up like that all day.'

'Why not?'

'You'll get egg down it at breakfast.'

'I for one shall have no time today to keep changing my clothes. Anyway, I can get one of those plastic bib things from the dental department. I must go across to St Swithin's right away, to see everyone's getting on their toes. Particularly the hospital engineer. Those damn automatic doors jammed again last night, of all things. And Oliphant telephoned me at midnight to say that he wasn't stuck in the lift.' The dean paused. 'I don't know why he did that. Perhaps he was being funny.'

The dean was back at seven-thirty for his breakfast. Like breakfast on any morning before such emotionally testing events as weddings, funerals and examinations, the atmosphere was tense and tetchy. All four residents of Number Two Lazar Row sat round the pink-topped table, preoccupied with their own concerns. Faith was wondering about Clem Undercroft. Auberon was contemplating Maggie M'Turk. Josephine was deeply worricd about which of her six specially bought hats finally to choose. And the dean was too bothered about everything to decide what to think about at all, but was overridingly obsessed with the weather.

'That damn television fellow was right for once,' he complained gloomily. He was swallowing strips of brown bread seeped in egg, covered from shoulders to knees with a sheet of blue plastic. 'It's suddenly clouded over. A most peculiar morning.'

'I should call it one with the freshness which reminds us that we can tire even of summer, yet heralding the narrow days of winter,' murmured Auberon, sitting in the dean's yellow Paisley dressing-gown and not looking up from reading the dean's morning paper. 'I expect if you went into the country and looked down the valleys, you'd see bride's veils of mist, twining and motionless.'

'What the devil are you talking about?' asked the dean crossly.

'The weather.'

The dean cracked his second egg, so urgently it exploded. 'Faith, my dear, I'm sorry that you can't be in the hall when Her Majesty arrives. Obviously, if all the consultants brought their entire families, the place would be like Oxford Circus tube station at the rush hour. Though I suppose I could have had you presented to the Queen, had I persevered. But Oliphant seemed to think you were a little too old for curtsying with a posy.'

'I shall watch from a window, daddy.'

'You'll find plenty of company. The entire nursing staff will be looking out of the front. God knows what happens if anyone wants a bedpan at the back.'

Joesphine sipped her coffee. 'I hope you can find a perch somewhere, too, Auberon. It does seem a pity to miss it, as you're so near.'

'Oh, I'll stroll over to the hospital. Of course, the whole show is a terrible bore. But it might be worth watching, on the chance that something might go quite spectacularly wrong.'

'I have always disliked your sense of humour,' the dean told him. 'But never quite so much as this morning.'

Auberon looked innocent. 'But I wasn't even being funny.'

'*Nothing* shall go wrong,' said the dean determinedly. 'I shall see to that.'

'I suppose you've checked the lightning conductors?' The dean looked worried. 'The architect may have forgotten to put them on. Often happens in new buildings. Everyone may be electrocuted.'

For the dean, the morning passed at the frantic, incident-packed speed of a television commercial. He was far too preoccupied even to notice the darkening of the sky. Then the consultants and their wives began to assemble in the hall, to him almost unrecognizable in their temporary splendour. Distinguished visitors started to arrive. There seemed to be policemen everywhere. Despite the crowd, the temperature suddenly dropped several degrees. Just before twelve came a flash and a whipcrack of thunder, and a screen of rain dropped abruptly beyond the opened glass doors.

'Oh, no!' cried the dean in horror. 'Just our bloody luck. The country's been bone dry since June, ruining all the farmers. And now the whole month's rainfall has to come in one morning.'

'Where's the special umbrella, Lionel?' asked Josephine anxiously beside him.

The dean searched round. 'It's up in my office. I've time to go up and fetch it.'

'Can't you send someone?'

'I'm sure that whoever I send will be quite capable of losing it and themselves, and have us all end up in the Tower.' Thunder again split the sky above the hospital. The rain fell even more ferociously. The dean looked at his watch hurriedly. It was six minutes to twelve. In just thirty-six minutes the Queen, with an unfailing punctuality quite beyond her Government's railways, would step from her car exactly outside the canopied front entrance.

'See no one pinches that blasted golden key,' he ordered Josephine. 'I wouldn't put anything at all past the St Swithin's students.'

The dean hurried to the lift.

He reached the top floor of the hospital. He turned right, and hurried down the corridor towards his office at the far end. As he expected, the anteroom was empty. His secretary would be already craning for a view somewhere. He snatched up the brand-new outsize umbrella from the corner by her filing cabinets, congratulating himself on his prudence in buying it during the previous week of blue skies. Canopy or not, it was essential no drop of rain could be risked to fall on the regal headgear which, for all the dean knew, might still have to do for some other important function like opening Parliament or reviewing the Fleet.

He unfurled the umbrella, opening it to make sure it contained no holes. Then he tried one or two royal-umbrella holding stances – arm bent, arm straight, elbow out, elbow in – walking several times across his secretary's office like the Guards doing the slow march at a funeral. He looked again at his watch. One minute past noon. Just twenty-nine minutes till Q hour. He rapidly furled the umbrella, and crooking it in his elbow hurried back to the closed doors of the lift.

The dean pressed the button. He waited. He pressed it again. He looked at his watch. Twelve two. He tapped his foot. He pressed the button once more. He tutted. He became aware of a muffled sound at the level of his feet.

He leant down, putting his ear to the crack between the sliding doors.

'For Christ's sake get us out of here,' said Professor Oliphant.

'Where are you?' asked the dean, aghast.

'Where do you think? In the bloody lift, of course. I am not hanging from my heels in the shaft pretending to be Dracula.'

'And it's stuck?'

'Of course it's stuck! I should have had more sense. I should have walked down the whole thirty storeys. I should have known that this piece of infernal machinery would obviously, unfailingly, utterly predictably and perfectly savagely, stick just when the Queen is about to walk into the place.'

The dean looked quickly right and left. No help in sight. 'How far have you got?'

'That is not a particularly helpful remark. If you must know, my face is on the level of your shoes. Now for God's sake do something.'

A high-pitched succession of squeaks came from the trapped lift. 'What's that?' asked the dean in alarm.

'I don't know, but it probably means "I can think of more pleasant ways of spending the morning" in Japanese. I am not alone in here,' Professor Oliphant continued steadily. 'I have the company of six eminent medical men from six different countries, none of whom speaks the language of any of the others, and certainly not mine. Also your uraemic sultan, who came along for the ride. Quite apart from anything else, this morning will see the end of the Common Market, if not of the United Nations.'

'But what am I to do?' the dean bleated.

'Go up to the blasted machine room,' shouted Professor Oliphant angrily. 'I showed you how to free the bloody thing when we were up there last Monday. You pull that red lever, which sticks out beyond the wheels in the far corner.'

'All right, all right.' Still with his umbrella, the dean started towards the door of the emergency stairs immediately to the side of the lift shaft. Feeling he should give some sort of encouragement to the hospital's guests in their plight, as an afterthought he shouted down, '*Ne pas se pencher dehors.*'

The machine room was on the floor immediately above. Just like Oliphant, the dean thought crossly as he pushed open the door, to make himself awkward at a moment like this. He peered round through his large glasses, trying to remember where the professor had demonstrated the essential red lever. He had to confess that he had not at the time followed with great concentration the Oliphant lecture on the disimpaction of lifts.

After fumbling for a precious minute, the dean spotted it. He gave a tug. There was instantly a whirring noise, and something warm splashed over him. For a horrified moment he thought it was blood – perhaps he had somehow mangled the lot of them in the machinery. But as he hurried into the light he saw that it was only oil. He clattered down the flight of steps, dabbing himself with his brand-new superior linen handkerchief. There safely on the top floor were the six foreign specialists, Professor Oliphant in morning dress, and the Sultan in pearl-studded robes and turban, all busily smoothing their rumpled clothes.

'I'm certainly not risking that lift again,' said the professor. 'We'll take the stairs – Good God, dean! You can't appear in front of the Queen like that.'

'It's only a spot or two of oil – '

'A spot! It's all over you. Great thick gobs of it. I warned you the other day, that place up there is packed with the filthy stuff. You look as though you should be on the boards at the Victoria Palace.'

The dean caught sight of his reflection in the glass panel of the emergency stairs door.

'Oh, my God,' he cried angrily. 'What am I going to do? And it's all your bloody fault.' He rounded on Professor Oliphant. 'It's only you who gets stuck in the blasted lift. Nobody else does. Not in the entire hospital. It strikes me that you have some quite abnormal way of pushing the button.'

'Don't blather, dean.' Professor Oliphant seized him by the arm. 'Fortunately, my decisive surgical mind has already formed an exact plan of action. But first I must get rid of this polyglot lot.'

The professor assumed a sickly smile, with his free hand pointing to the emergency stairs and making plunging motions downward. 'You down. See? Me up. Savvy? Me – ' He indicated himself. 'Stay with dean.' He jabbed the dean hard on the chest to make his meaning perfectly clear. '*Compris?*'

His foreign colleagues nodded and smiled. They clattered away down the stone steps, for thirty storeys. 'Come on.' Professor Oliphant marched the dean after them. 'I'll have the situation restored to normal in no time.'

'Where are we going?' asked the dean piteously. 'There's barely another twenty-five minutes before Her actual Majesty appears.'

'Don't worry.' Professor Oliphant gripped his arm the tighter as they started down the emergency stairs. 'Twenty-five minutes? Why, that's an age. I could relieve a couple of people of their appendices by then. We are going to my operating theatre suite on the twenty-ninth floor, just below. Naturally, it is not in use today, and completely deserted. There you will go to my personal shower – which since my complaint I am delighted to say is not fed exclusively with superheated steam. Your morning suit is thankfully almost unspotted. Stow it in the clothes locker and wash that muck off you with some skin detergent. It'll take about half a minute. You'll be in plenty of time to be back on parade as if nothing had happened. Indeed, looking all the better and fresher. I only wish I'd had enough sense to take a quick shower too, this sticky weather.'

'What a brilliant idea!' exclaimed the dean. They reached the floor below. 'And it all seems so simple!

I don't know why I was so worried a moment ago.'

'In surgery, my dear dean, we grow used to handling emergencies at a second's notice.'

'I really am most awfully grateful to you, Gerry.'

'Not a bit, dean.'

They reached the small door beside the theatres marked PROFESSOR OF SURGERY ONLY. 'We may have had our disagreements in the past, Gerry – '

'Have we, dean? I can hardly remember any.'

'Our personality clashes, possibly. Inevitable, with two men of brilliance and forceful outlook.'

'Quite understandable, dean. Irresistible forces and immovable posts.'

'But after this, my dear Gerry, I'd like you to think that we were . . . well, firm chums.'

'My dear dean, I should shake you warmly by the hand, if it wasn't in such a filthy state.' The professor opened the door. 'There's the shower. Here's the detergent. I'll nip below and reassure Josephine and everyone else that all is absolutely under control, and you'll be down in about five minutes, ready for your big act.' He looked at his watch. 'Why, you've got a good fifteen minutes' leeway, unless you linger in the shower and start singing or something. By the way, dean – '

'Yes, Gerry?'

'Must you take that umbrella in the shower with you? It would seem likely to invalidate the entire exercise.'

The dean looked with surprise at the umbrella on his arm. 'It's for the Queen's hat. Take it down, there's a good chap, and keep it handy for me.'

Alone, the dean quickly stripped off his clothes, pushed them into the waterproof locker provided for the purpose, turned on the shower, gingerly tested the temperature with his finger tips, stepped inside, and lavishly soaped himself with detergent used in the theatres for cleansing and sterilizing the patients' skins on the operating table. He was clean in a few seconds. Wasting no time, he found a towel at the bottom of another locker, rubbed himself briskly, and pushed it down the laundry chute. He picked up his glasses from the soap dish. He turned to regain his clothes. An inch away from the handle of the locker, he froze. He grabbed the handle, pulling it open. Empty. He tugged open the laundry chute. Naturally, empty.

'Oh, my God,' muttered the dean. Every stitch was thirty storeys below in the basement, at that moment doubtless being churned in the electronically operated automatic washing machines.

20

'ARE you sure it's going to be all right?' asked Faith, more in excitement that it would rather than fear that it wouldn't.

'Of course it will.' Holding her hand tightly, Clem Undercroft looked warily from the lift doors opening on to the thirtieth floor at St Swithin's. He was still in his white coat, glasses more askew than ever.

'But why can't we simply go to your room in the residents' quarters?' she protested.

'How did I know the place would be crawling with policemen? Anyway, this is just as good. Better if anything.'

'But supposing Professor Oliphant comes in?'

'Not the remotest possibility.' Clem tugged her away to the left, along the top floor corridor. The lift doors slid together behind them. 'I saw Ollie down in the hall just now. He was busy with all those funny people he keeps taking round the hospital and waving his arms at.'

'What are we going to do it *on*?' asked Faith, who had a practical mind, like her father.

'Everyone knows Ollie has got himself a nice little bedroom up here in his office. Trust him to look after number one. He says so he can be on hand for emergencies, as they wouldn't give him a cheap house in Lazar Row like your dad. I've seen the place. Comfy divan. Loo. Even a bidet. I don't know what he does with it. We might find something to drink, too.'

She squeezed his hand. 'You *are* clever, Clem. Such a pity Daddy doesn't appreciate it.'

As the couple disappeared silently through the door of Professor Oliphant's office, the lift doors slid apart again.

'Are you sure it's going to be all right?' asked Auberon, more in fear that it wouldn't rather than excitement that it would.

'Of course it will.' Dr M'Turk gripped his hand tightly. She was wearing a short dress of purple velvet, her hair in place with a length of golden chain. 'Everyone's gawping at the Queen.' Auberon looked nervously up and down the empty corridor. 'What else are you worrying about?' she demanded.

'Your husband.'

'Oh, him.' Dr M'Turk gave an impatient gesture. 'He's half way across London at the Soho Clinic, operating on some transvestites. Just put him out of your mind, dear. Come on.'

They entered the familiar consulting room. Dr M'Turk locked the door behind them, taking out the key and holding it up. 'Less nervy now?' she smiled.

'You must think me rather ridiculously on edge.'

She laid the key on the desk next to the bust of Freud. 'Not a bit. It's flattering. It shows you don't do this sort of thing every day.'

'Well, not in a hospital. That bothers me a bit. It seems a little inappropriate. Like eating sweets in church.'

She had her arms round his neck, her eyes shut, her lips open, pressing hard against him. 'Relax, darling, relax . . . we're alone . . . up here, we could be ultimately anonymous on some high mountain peak, our only witness the winsome wind.'

'I said that in *Slits*.'

'Take me. . . .' She ripped off her purple dress.

'You look so lovely in your Freudian slip,' he murmured.

'Take me. . . .' The rest of her clothes disappeared into one corner. Auberon kicked off his shoes, trousers and Y-fronts, throwing them with his shirt and jacket into another.

'Take me *now*. . . .' Dr M'Turk fell backwards on to the consulting couch. Auberon fell on to Dr M'Turk. They lay breathing fiercely, hands running over each other like hungry mice, lips crushing lips like squeezed oranges, their bodies pressed together with the violent impact of long-suppressed passion. The door opened and her husband came in.

'Hamish!' Dr M'Turk sat up with a screech.

'Hello, there,' said Auberon dazedly. 'Haven't we met?'

'How did you get in?' she demanded crossly.

'With a key.' Hamish M'Turk smiled, shutting the consulting-room door behind him. 'A spare key. *Your* spare key, my dear. From the key-ring which you keep in your desk in our sitting-room.' He held it up. 'I was possessed with a most unworthy suspicion this morning, I'm afraid, that one key at least might be missing.' He laid his key carefully on the desk beside the other. 'You seem to forget, my love, that I am a trained sexologist. Besides, you have had for years an unfortunate tendency to talk in your sleep.' He leant against the edge of the desk, arms folded, still smiling. 'And furthermore, my sweetheart, whatever may be your own opinion, I am no fool.'

'Hamish, you mustn't get the wrong impression. This is Mr Dougal's treatment.'

'Indeed? More agreeable, I should imagine, than swallowing lots of pills.'

'You know perfectly well that sex therapy is well established in America.'

'*Established*, my darling? Let us say that those enthusiastic, active Americans have a touching fondness for any exculpatory doctrine in modern psychiatry.'

'Hamish!' She looked horrified. 'You're going bourgeois.'

'What do you mean? That I should sit on this uncomfortable perch watching this anaemic pseudo-intellectual hack writer rodgering you? With enjoyment? Perhaps even cheering encouragement from time to time?'

'You know perfectly well we've discussed this endlessly. That marriage isn't simply a life sentence of emotional solitary confinement.'

'*You've* discussed it endlessly. I can't remember my own opinions being invited on that particular topic.'

She gave an outraged stare. 'This is a fine time to tell me you deny the existence of sexual freedom.'

'Only *your* sexual freedom, my charmer.' He continued to smile. 'And I know all about it, too. These last few years you've been having it off more often than a striptease dancer's bra. But *I* haven't. On the occasion – the single occasion – when you found me taking that pretty little redheaded theatre nurse out for dinner, you stormed about the house for weeks.'

'Well, she was a little bitch and bad for you,' Dr M'Turk told him briefly. 'Furthermore, it is extremely undignified, going about snooping on me like this. You've upset Mr Dougal tremendously.'

'Please don't bother yourself about my feelings.' said Auberon, who had been gazing at Hamish with intense anxiety. 'I don't mind a bit. Honestly.'

Dr M'Turk made a movement from the couch. 'I'm going home.'

'Stay where you are.' Hamish's smile vanished. 'Both of you.'

From his inside pocket he drew a plastic sheath. From the sheath he took a surgical scalpel.

'What . . . what are you going to do?' Dr M'Turk asked faintly.

'An operation.' He gave Auberon a fierce look. 'Just a little operation.'

'Oh, no!' Auberon leapt up, hands over his groin. Hamish M'Turk advanced quickly, scalpel gleaming like a bayonet.

'Just a little operation, my friend,' Hamish continued grimly. 'Why, you'll hardly notice it. It's perfectly safe. The mortality rate is nil, I assure you. And convalescence is generally quite uncomplicated. I'm performing it every day on incorrigible sex offenders. Just a quick snick . . . and another quick snick. Then your sexual problems will disappear. Just disappear. For ever and ever.'

'No, no, please! Honestly, it was Maggie who suggested it – '

'One day you'll thank me for this little operation, my dear friend. Your bestial desires will melt into thin air. It will spare you heaven knows what troubles with the law and society in the future. You might become quite nice to know. It's amazing what can be done to a man with a slight snick – '

Auberon jumped behind the couch. With a snarl, Hamish leapt after him. Auberon backed into the corner. The surgeon followed, flashing his scalpel. Dr M'Turk grabbed both keys from the desk. She picked up the bust of Freud. Taking careful aim, she swung it at her husband, catching him in the nape of the neck.

'Quick!' Her husband staggered against the wall. She dropped the bust and grabbed Auberon's hand. They flew through the door. She locked it behind them, throwing both keys through the swing door of the emergency stairs, hearing them clatter downwards.

'But all our clothes are in there,' Auberon complained frantically.

'*You* go and fetch them, if you want to.'

He cast his eyes up and down his own naked body, then hers. 'We can't go wandering about the hospital like this. Even the patients have some sort of nightshirts, haven't they?'

'Don't make difficulties.' Dr M'Turk started to drag him along the corridor, to the left of the lift. 'This way.'

'Where are we going?' he asked nervously.

'The professor of surgery's office. I happen to know he's got a bedroom attached to it. We'll be able to find something. A couple of white coats, at least.'

Angry thumps shook the locked consulting-room door. Glancing in panic over his shoulder and shivering violently, Auberon let Dr M'Turk hurry him along the corridor. 'But supposing the professor's in there?' he objected. 'I met him yesterday – a fearsome character, he scared the daylights out of me. I can't see him co-operating much.'

'He'll be downstairs,' she told him impatiently. 'Waiting for the Queen.'

'Oh, my God! I'd forgotten that.'

Dr M'Turk opened the outer door of Professor Oliphant's office. As she flung open an inner one, the naked bodies of Faith and Clem pulled violently apart.

'Well!' exclaimed Dr M'Turk.

'Oh!' cried Faith in disappointment. 'And we hadn't started properly yet, either.'

'Who the hell are you?' Dr M'Turk demanded of Clem.

'S-S-S-Sir Lionel Lychfield's house physician.' He was still wearing his glasses, almost vertical on his face.

'Taking your job rather seriously, aren't you?'

'Why, it's Uncle Auberon,' exclaimed Faith. 'Hello, uncle. How come you haven't any clothes on?'

'Don't ask questions,' Dr M'Turk told her crisply. 'We were having sunlamp treatment in the dermatology department. We suffer from acne. Both of us. All over.'

'Yes, and the department caught fire,' Auberon added quickly. 'We had to leave instantly. To save our skins, as it were.'

'Give me those clothes.' Dr M'Turk pointed determinedly to the pile of male and female garments at the foot of the professor's divan.

'Not on your life,' said Clem, grabbing them.

'Come on. Or I'll tell on you both.'

'So shall I on you,' said Faith.

'They'd never fit you,' Clem added desperately.

'Come on.' Dr M'Turk advanced, eyes glinting. 'Give.'

'Why should we be the ones to land in trouble,' and not you two?' Clem demanded defiantly, clutching the garments to him.

'Good boy, now,' said Dr M'Turk. 'Drop it. Drop – Ouch! You little bitch.'

Faith had bitten her hard on the forearm.

Clem leapt for the door, tripping over his own dangling trousers, dropping half the bundle in panic. Faith dashed into the corridor after him. She was followed closely by Auberon, clutching at the trailing sleeve of Clem's white coat, and Dr M'Turk holding her bleeding arm. At that moment the dean, having found nothing more helpful in the operating theatres than a pack of finger dressings, was advancing in the nude warily from the door of the emergency staircase in the direction of his office.

21

'FAITH!'

'Daddy!'

'Undercroft!'

'Sir.'

'Auberon!'

'Hello, there!'

'And Dr M'Turk!'

'Sir Lionel, you've got to do something.'

The dean stared. 'I'm dreaming.' He pinched his bare thigh. 'Yes, it's that dream again. That awfully common dream. Where everybody's got no clothes on. I'll wake up in a minute. I'll be in bed in my spotted pyjamas, with Josephine. I'll go down as usual, and have my boiled eggs for breakfast – ' He broke off. 'What's that terrible thumping noise?'

'My husband,' Dr M'Turk told him impatiently.

'In your clinic?' The dean looked mystified through his large round glasses, with his waterproof wristwatch his only costume. 'What's he doing in your clinic? He hasn't come for treatment, has he?'

'Please don't ask me to go into that now, Sir Lionel. We've got to find some clothes.'

'*You* have to! What about me, for God's sake? My entire career, my entire life is already ruined. In precisely – ' he looked at his watch. 'Eight minutes I am expected to welcome to the hospital Her Majesty the Queen. I think even the most liberal minded of modern progressive thinkers might agree that it would not be entirely desirable for me to do so like this. So Her Majesty will simply stand about downstairs waiting for someone to hand her a golden key. "Where's Lychfield?" she'll ask. And no one will know. They will simply look at each other in embarrassment for several minutes, then all melt away. The Queen will have to go back to the Palace, with nothing to do till tea. A whole afternoon ruined. I've got about as much chance now of seeing the inside of the Royal Household as seeing the inside of the Kremlin,' he continued resignedly. 'My residual hope was being able to cover myself with my secretary's macintosh from her office. Though now I seem to recall even that is of transparent plastic.'

'But daddy, where *are* your clothes?' demanded Faith. 'You had them all on when you left home after breakfast.'

'Good question. To which – My, my, Faith, you *are* getting a big girl, aren't you? To which I can reply briefly. They are in the hospital laundry. Going by the usual standard of service from that department, I shan't see them again for a month. And if *I* may ask, what are you doing yourself in that state, my girl?' The dean's voice hardened. 'And furthermore, what sort of coincidence is it that my addle-brained houseman – good God, Undercroft, I'd no idea that mild exterior covered such remarkable physique – is also walking about stark naked in broad daylight?'

'We were stopped and searched, daddy. By the security police. They were ever so thorough. Then unfortunately the air conditioning sucked our clothes into the ventilation shaft. Like you said happened to all Professor Oliphant's important letters. I think Uncle Auberon and Dr M'Turk were sharing a sun-lamp.'

The dean passed a hand wearily across his forehead. 'I am beyond bothering any longer about such minor things. For months I've worked myself to death getting ready to greet the Queen. Now all is wasted, wasted. All that energy squandered! My little speech, into which I put so much care, so much effort, so much polishing. . . .' His voice broke. 'It is no more than a poem shouted to the wind.'

He stopped. There was a whirring noise from the lift. All five nudes looked at each other.

'Someone's coming up,' muttered Auberon.

'Coming right up here,' added Dr M'Turk.

'My God,' muttered the dean in horror. 'It *can't* be the Queen?'

The whirr stopped. The doors slid apart. Out stepped the Reverend Thomas Arnold Becket, in gleaming clerical collar, brilliant royal blue stock, impeccable tail coat, razor-creased striped trousers and double-breasted dove-grey waistcoat.

The hospital chaplain stopped short. He stared. He blinked. His eyes rolled. His lips moved. 'I'm dead,' he muttered. 'Some disaster has struck the hospital. While I was coming up in the lift. It was hit by lightning. We are all enjoying the life eternal. We are in Heaven.' He bowed courteously in the direction of the dean. 'How do you do, Sir Lionel. How nice to be with you for ever.'

'Where did you get those clothes?' hissed the dean.

The chaplain stared down at himself. 'Moss Bros.'

'I mean, you didn't find them in the hospital laundry?'

The chaplain looked offended. 'Of course I didn't. I know you make mock of my usual gear, but I only wear it so's people will accept me as an ordinary bloke. I can dress to fit the occasion, like now. I don't know what's going on here,' he continued, even more confused. 'I only know that Professor Oliphant sent me up to see what had happened to the dean.'

'Take them off.' The dean advanced on the chaplain.

'What!'

'Take those clothes off. All of them. Every stitch. You have exactly fifteen seconds to divest yourself.'

The chaplain looked round wildly. 'I pray you, have some respect for my cloth. You can hardly expect me to join your love-in, or whatever orgy you happen to be holding. At, I might say, a very peculiar time, all considered.'

More hammering came from the door opposite the lift, with snarls of, 'I'll murder you, Maggie! I'll cut you up. Into little bits. You'll end up pickled in a row of jars in the hospital museum.'

'Off,' commanded the dean. 'Off, off.'

'Here! Take your hands away.'

'Off. Off! Come along, Undercroft. And you, Auberon. Don't just stand there. Give me a hand.'

'Come on, everyone,' invited Faith, leaping forward. 'It's time poor daddy had a break. Let's undress the chaplain.'

Ten seconds, and the dean was holding up the chaplain's trousers.

'The collar's going to be a bit of a problem,' he was murmuring thoughtfully. 'But I suppose I can turn it round somehow. I do hope the Queen won't notice I'm wearing a rather peculiar royal blue tie.'

From the door of the dean's office, eyes shut, arms outstretched like a sleepwalker, Mrs Samantha Dougal came towards the lift with no clothes on.

'Good God,' exclaimed the dean. 'Now I've got it. We're all gripped with some form of mass hysteria. It's like the Devils of Loudun.'

Mrs Samantha Dougal stopped. She opened her eyes. 'I *am* mad,' she gasped. 'I don't have to pretend. I am.'

'Hello, Samantha,' said the dean, eyeing her up and down. 'How nice.'

'Samantha!'

'Auberon!'

They clasped with bare arms.

'Samantha, I *am* glad to see you!'

'Yes dear, I can observe that.'

'Samantha, my darling, I want to come back.'

'Auberon my lover, I've been so utterly wretched without you.'

'I'll never leave you again. Never! I don't mean just over the next six months, I promise.'

'And I promise never to mention again the sanctity of marriage.'

'Samantha, my sweet, I *know* I write potboilers.'

'But Auberon, my angel, they are the most lovely potboilers in the world.'

'Don't bother a damn about this stupid shoplifting business.'

'I shan't. I'm giving up morality for good. I shall take up the pollution of the environment instead.'

'How do I look?' the dean pulled proudly at his lapels.

'It's an excellent fit, daddy,' said Faith proudly.

'I agree. Moss Bros really are amazingly good value.'

'Why, there's the hospital chaplain,' said Mrs Samantha Dougal. The Reverend Becket was trying to hide behind the angular frame of Dr M'Turk. 'Are you preaching perhaps a little too thoroughly on the parable of the Good Samaritan?'

'I am *not* the hospital chaplain. I am the ex-chaplain. I am resigning, Mrs Dougal. I never did like this job for a start. As a matter of fact, I can't even stand hospitals. The smell of them makes me feel sick. I'm going to a prison, where at least they don't tear the clothes off your back.'

The dean looked at his watch again. 'What perfect timing! I have exactly two minutes. Now if everyone will kindly excuse me, I must leave you. I think under the circumstances I had better risk taking the lift. It is unlikely to break down twice in the same morning, on the principle that lightning never strikes in the same spot — '

The dean broke off. He looked through the window at the end of the corridor. The rain had stopped. The clouds had rolled away. A golden glow filled the building. 'Why, it's a perfectly lovely day now. Well, I must be getting along.'

'The sun – ' Auberon snapped his fingers. 'Like a great custard pie in the sky.'

The dean went down. The lift didn't stick. Everyone agreed afterwards that Her Majesty had never been more gracious, charming or radiant.

MORE ABOUT PENGUINS AND PELICANS

Penguinews, which appears every month, contains details of all the new books issued by Penguins as they are published. From time to time it is supplemented by *Penguins in Print*, which is a complete list of all titles available. (There are some five thousand of these.)

A specimen copy of *Penguinews* will be sent to you free on request. For a year's issues (including the complete lists) please send £1.00 if you live in the British Isles, or elsewhere. Just write to Dept EP, Penguin Books Ltd, Hardmondsworth, Middlesex, enclosing a cheque or postal order, and your name will be added to the mailing list.

In the U.S.A.: For a complete list of books available from Penguin in the United States write to Dept CS, Penguin Books Inc., 7110 Ambassador Road, Baltimore, Maryland 21207.

In Canada: For a complete list of books available from Penguin in Canada write to Penguin Books Canada Ltd, 41 Steelcase Road West, Markham, Ontario.

H. E. BATES'S BEST-SELLING 'LARKIN' BOOKS

THE DARLING BUDS OF MAY

Introducing the Larkins, a family with a place in popular mythology.

Here they come, in the first of their hilarious rural adventures, crashing their way through the English countryside in the wake of Pa, the quick-eyed golden-hearted junk-dealer, and Ma, with a mouthful of crisps and a laugh like a jelly.

A BREATH OF FRENCH AIR

They're here again – the indestructible Larkins; this time, with Baby Oscar, the Rolls, and Ma's unmarried passport, they're off to France. And with H. E. Bates, you may be sure, there's no French without tears of laughter.

WHEN THE GREEN WOODS LAUGH

In the third of the Larkin novels H. E. Bates makes the Dragon's Blood and the double scotches hit with no less impact than they did in *The Darling Buds of May*. For the full Larkin orchestra is back on the rural fiddle, and (with Angela Snow around) the Brigadier may be too old to ride but he's young enough to fall.

OH! TO BE IN ENGLAND

Are you taking life too seriously?

What you need is a dose of *Oh! To Be in England* – another splendid thighs-breasts-and-buttercups frolic through the Merrie England of the sixties with the thirsty, happy, lusty, quite uninhibited and now rightly famous junk-dealing family of Larkins.

and

A Little of What You Fancy

RICHARD GORDON

'His books are like an injection of elixir' – *Manchester Evening News*

'One reads throughout with a gentle smile that breaks occasionally into a bark of laughter at some unexpected ribaldry or asperity' – *Sunday Times*

'Rich and racy humour and a shrewd and sympathetic understanding' – *Scotsman*

'The golden formula . . . grafting Wodehouse on to the *Lancet*' – *New Statesman*

'Sheer unadulterated fun' – *Star*

The following titles have been published in Penguins:

DOCTOR AT SEA

DOCTOR IN THE HOUSE

DOCTOR IN LOVE

DOCTOR ON THE BRAIN

DOCTOR AND SON

DOCTOR AT LARGE

DOCTOR IN CLOVER

DOCTOR IN THE SWIM

DOCTOR ON THE BOIL

DOCTOR ON TOAST